IN
TOO
DEEP

To Caleb and Rocco, my own little blessings

JANETTA OTTER-BARRY BOOKS

In Too Deep copyright © Frances Lincoln Limited 2013
Text copyright © Tom Avery 2013

First published in Great Britain in 2013 by
Frances Lincoln Children's Books, 4 Torriano Mews,
Torriano Avenue, London NW5 2RZ

www.franceslincoln.com

A catalogue record for this book is available from the British Library.

ISBN 978-1-84780-389-4

Set in Palatino

Printed and bound by CPI Group (UK) Ltd, Croydon, CR0 4YY

1 3 5 7 9 8 6 4 2

IN
TOO
DEEP

TOM AVERY

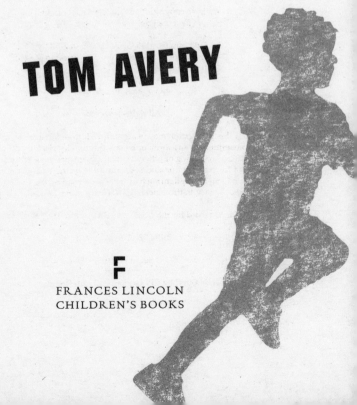

F
FRANCES LINCOLN
CHILDREN'S BOOKS

Chapter 1

Eastern Katanga, Democratic Republic of Congo, four years ago

We ran until the sweat poured down our faces, until our lungs burned and the dust we kicked up hung thick in the air. We chased the hard brown ball, desperate to keep it at our feet. Taunting doubled the fun.

'You won't catch me this time, Prince,' hollered my brother, two years older than me and a few inches taller, as he skipped away.

Emmanuel was good, but my dadda was better. He laughed and laughed as he threaded the ball between our legs, flicked it over our heads and spun past us.

'Come on, you slow-coaches!' he called in his deep voice.

That's how we used to play football, my dadda, Emmanuel and me.

I remember the last time we all played together. I remember it well. The red African sun was beating down as fiercely as ever, the sweat running. After a long game, we collapsed on to the ground, me and Emmanuel either side of my father.

'You know, boys,' Dadda reached out and took hold of our hands, 'I'll never let anything bad happen to you.'

Nothing bad? Nothing bad? Since my dad uttered those words a lot has happened. Emmanuel and I have been sent away, abandoned and homeless. We've been runaways, thieves and gang members. We've fended for ourselves. And I'm only eleven.

I thought a lot about what I would say to my father if we met again. But when it comes to it, what we plan to say and what comes out of our mouths are two very different things.

Chapter 2

I don't like sitting still as much as my brother.

When we met up, every other week, he loved to sit. Just sit and talk – on our beds, on our foster carers' sofas, on a park bench. He said that he was making up for all the times he couldn't sit down, all the times he had to run, all the times we were on the move.

We played a lot of football as well, just me and Emmanuel. We played the same way as we used to – chasing the ball, chasing each other, keeping the ball as long as we could. I usually kept it a lot longer than my brother. The ball was white, with a big black tick on it, and the ground was covered with green grass; no dust in the air.

The park across the road from Ruth and Jubrel's, my foster family, was a long way from our dusty home in Africa, long in distance and long in time. Just scraps of memories remained of our home, of my mother and father, of my family. Apart from Em of course, my brother.

I've told you about the last time we played with our dadda. Now I'll tell you about the last time we played in that park.

We were wrapped up warm, in hats that came down over our ears, their furry lining soft against our skin, flapping as we ran. We didn't talk much as we played, it was too cold; our jaws were locked shut, trying to keep the heat in. I tried to talk, if shouting insults at your brother counts as talking. Emmanuel didn't reply, he just laughed. I loved to hear my brother laugh. Somehow it made me feel warmer.

Over the years I had got better and better at football. I played on the school team and for a club outside school. There was only one kid as good as me, and that was George, my best friend. I kicked a ball around with George even more than I did with my brother. Emmanuel had stopped playing really, unless you counted our fortnightly kick-abouts. He went to a secondary school now. He told me they didn't do much sport at his school.

When we had run for maybe twenty minutes Emmanuel stopped, coughed and said, 'It's too cold for this.'

I flicked the ball up into my hands. The white plastic stung my frozen skin as I caught it. 'Come on,' I said, 'ten more minutes.'

'Nah, let's get a drink or something.' Emmanuel beckoned and I followed. My brother was in charge these days and I stayed as close to him as I could. I thought I'd lost him once. I didn't want that to happen again.

There was a little shop in the park that sold frothy hot drinks in the winter and tons of ice-creams in the summer. You could buy chocolate and fizzy drinks any time.

We stood in line behind a woman in a headscarf and a tall boy with a large smile. They were both black, like us. I guessed they were Somali. Some of my friends at school came from Somalia.

Emmanuel and I had a game we liked to play. When we saw some interesting people, one of us would say, 'What about them?' Then the other would try to think of their names and invent some of their story. Alice, Em's foster carer, had taught us to do it.

She said it would help us to think about other people and understand that everyone has feelings, and stuff like that. Alice loved talking about feelings. I think Em had begun to love it too. He said it was important, but he didn't answer when I asked why.

The mother and son bought a chocolate bar. When the mother had paid for it she gave it impatiently to the boy and said something in another language. Then they hurried away. I love not understanding different languages. I love the mystery.

'What about those two?' I said to my brother.

Emmanuel had already asked the shop-keeper for two bottles of fizzy orange drink. He paid and thanked the man, before turning to watch the boy and his mum hurry towards the park gate.

'Erm . . .' He thought for a moment and handed me a drink. 'He's called Ali, she's . . . I don't know. He's got five big brothers and sisters.' He paused again as the pair reached the park exit. I opened my bottle of drink with a hiss. 'His dad is a doctor. . . '

'And his oldest brother is going to be a doctor too,' I added.

Emmanuel finished, 'And they live in one of the big houses on Leighton Grove.'

'Where's that?' I asked, swigging my drink.

'You know, it's near your school. All the kids come out in posh uniforms and it's lined with proper shiny cars.'

'Nice,' I replied.

We walked as we talked, Emmanuel leading the way, and arrived at one of our favourite benches. We sat. I thought about those big houses and shiny cars and guzzled down my drink. Then Em said, 'What d'you think of those two?' He pointed at a boy, about eight or nine, and a man I guessed was his dad. They were running around on the football pitch, passing an oval rugby ball back and forth. A grin was stretched across the boy's face.

'They got money,' I said. 'They look minted. Check out those pearly whites.' I pointed to the boy's fresh trainers, then looked down at my own scuffed, greying shoes, now spattered with mud.

'So what?' Emmanuel replied. 'It's not all about money, Prince.'

'Everything's about money.' I threw my empty bottle towards a nearby bin as I said this. It hit the rim and bounced off on to the grass. I groaned, and stood up to retrieve it. 'You've got money,' I said, 'and you're happy.' I had another shot at the bin and the bottle sailed in this time. 'You've not got money,

11

and you're not happy.'

Emmanuel turned his whole body to look at me and put his foot up on the bench between us. 'You think you can't be happy without money?'

I thought about that for a while. I wasn't sure. I looked at the grinning boy running around with his dad, whose gold watch glinted in the sun as he caught the muddy ball.

'Money equals happiness,' I replied. 'We've never had any, that's why we've never been happy.'

'I'm happy,' Emmanuel said. I could feel him staring at the side of my head as he said this. I was still intent on the boy and his father – they were wrestling with the ball now.

I looked at my brother. 'You're happy?' I said.

Em nodded, then stood up to put his empty bottle in the bin.

I looked back at the father and son. They were laughing, the ball forgotten on the ground.

'I'm not,' I whispered.

Chapter 3

Ilala Market, Dar Es Salaam, Tanzania

Many, many miles away, darkness began to fall on my father, Céléstin Anatole. A tall man, wiry, tough, he stood behind a table. The table was missing a leg and rested against his body. Céléstin daren't move in case it collapsed and everything on it scattered across the dusty ground.

He looked down. The table, covered with a tattered cloth, held a disparate collection of bracelets and clothing plus a pair of crushed and battered running shoes. Every unsold item was a bitter reminder of the debt he must repay.

Most stalls in this section of Ilala market were stocked, like Céléstin's, with second-hand 'odds and ends' gathered from across the city. And many of the stall-holders were in debt, like him. They owed every penny they made to local businessmen, if the qualification of being a businessman is wearing a suit and having more money than the people around you. If, however, the qualification is the kind of work you do, then my father owed his debt to gangsters and smugglers.

Céléstin missed his home. Lake Tanganyika was over five hundred miles away and his home in Katanga even further. But no matter how much he missed it, he'd never return. Everything he missed was gone, replaced by violence and fear.

'How's business?'

Céléstin, expecting a visit from his debt collectors, shifted suddenly, coughed loudly, and half his wares tumbled to the floor as the table slouched.

'Ah, sorry,' said his friend, Godwin, a fellow stall-holder, bending to pick up the scattered jewellery and clothing. 'I did not mean to surprise you. Your cough's getting worse than my old father's, my friend.' Godwin was always quick with a joke and he looked up with a twinkle in his eye as he replaced the merchandise.

Whilst the market moved from tables and stalls

into brown and broken suitcases and the last customers headed home, the two men, dressed in cream-coloured Kanzu and black jackets, swapped stories of the day's trading and shared a handful of spicy roast nuts.

The Kanzu, a long dress that gathered the city's dirt like a fly trap, along with the Kofia cap, was not familiar to Céléstin. The polyester made him sweat under the hot sun and by the end of the day he felt just like his table – ready to tumble. But without them, he found it hard to sell anything to the local hagglers. He did all he could to fit in. He spoke the little Swahili he had learnt in every greeting, he ate the local food. It was all part of working hard, all part of earning money and paying off the debt.

'Have you heard anything?' The two men's talk turned to important matters.

'Nothing,' Céléstin replied. 'But I don't expect to, not for a while, at least.'

'You think she made it, though.'

Céléstin let out another hacking cough before he replied. 'They tell me she did.' "They" were the nefarious businessmen to whom my father owed his debt. He ran a hand over his greying hair. 'And I trust.' Just a few short years ago his hair had been jet black. They say that pain and anguish turn the hair grey.

Godwin cracked a wry smile. 'Your faith is vast indeed if you trust them.'

Céléstin shook his head. 'I do not trust them. I trust Him,' he said, pointing heavenwards. Another spate of coughing ruined his sad smile.

Chapter 4

We got back to Ruth and Jubrel's a bit late. Alice was waiting to take Em home. They didn't live far away, Emmanuel and Alice, two bus rides. But Alice said she liked to pick him up. I think my brother liked it too.

'Come on then, Manny,' Alice said. That's what she called Emmanuel, Manny. Funny, right? People think my name is funny too. I get loads of nicknames, mostly from teachers. The French teacher always sings this song about purple rain that's got something to do with my name. Miss Strong, my class teacher, sometimes says, 'Farewell, sweet Prince.' My friends mostly just call me Princey.

I grabbed my brother in a hug and said goodbye. I waved from the porch as Em got into Alice's little green car.

The front door closed behind me and Ruth smiled, a small grin painted across her dark face. 'You have a nice time?' she asked.

Ruth had a strong Nigerian accent, not like Jubrel, who was from the same country as me and Em, the Democratic Republic of Congo. That's why they decided I should live with the Milandus, because Jubrel knew all about where we'd come from. But maybe, I had begun to think, knowing where you've come from isn't as important as knowing the journey you've been on. Luckily Jubrel was pretty good at understanding that too.

'Yeah, it was good,' I replied. 'Not enough football though.'

Ruth laughed. She knew that I would play football every moment I could.

'Dinner in about an hour, OK?' she said.

I groaned, pressing my hands to my stomach.

Ruth rolled her eyes. 'You boys are always hungry,' she said with a smile, before promising to bring me 'a little something' before dinner.

As Ruth headed towards the kitchen I kicked off

my shoes and threw my coat at the coat stand.

'Pick them up, Princey,' Ruth called.

I quickly picked up my shoes and placed them on the rack, not tidy, but in the right place at least. My coat had stayed, bundled on top of the stand, so I left it. I ran into the front room and flicked on the television. I crashed down onto my bean-bag.

Ruth and Jubrel had all the sports channels. It was brilliant – there was always football on. I watched some Italian teams playing, 'an important match', the commentator kept telling me. Both teams were good, and it was hard to choose who to support. In the end I went for the team in black-and-white stripes. They had the cooler kit.

I had only been watching for a few minutes when Ruth brought me peanut butter on toast, my favourite snack. She laughed and made a joke about me being 'an obsessive-compulsive'. I think she meant I watched too much football and probably ate too much peanut butter.

It was only highlights, the football, so it didn't last long. Neither did the toast. The plate lay abandoned at my feet when I flicked channels, and I found myself watching the news. Boring. I didn't often pay attention to the news, not like my brother. He loved to know what was going on in the world.

On that afternoon, there was a famine in some country in Africa. Apparently the government wasn't running the country properly or something. It looked really sad. The people were living in tents and the kids had flies all over them.

As you know, I lived in Africa once upon a time, but I don't remember much. I just remember football, my school and the town near our house. I remember that it was hot.

I also remember my mum's singing and my dad's laughter; I used to hear those all the time. When I am halfway between being awake and asleep, when thoughts and daydreams have passed but real dreams have not begun, those are the sounds I hear, my father's deep chuckle and my mother's sing-song tones. Every night I hear them, and then fleeting memories play in my mind's eye. I love those moments.

After the news report it went to the weather. I was just about to switch channels when the doorbell rang.

I leapt up and hurtled into the hall. Ruth's favourite radio station was playing in the kitchen; I could just hear her humming along.

'You got it, Prince?' She called.

I replied with a 'yeah' as I turned the handle.

Facing me was a lady with white hair, as white as Alice's, like a covering of frost. If you looked at her face she didn't look old, but her hair made her look ancient. She was carrying a leather bag over her shoulder and she had an ID card pinned to her green cardigan. I recognised her.

When your parents aren't around or you're in trouble for some other reason, you have social workers. They're people who make sure that you're OK, a bit like all the aunties that some of my friends at school had. They dug around in your life, checked you weren't in trouble, asked teachers about you, that kind of stuff. Part of me loved having the social workers. After all, they cared. Part of me hated it. After all, they weren't my parents.

This lady was a social worker. Not my social worker, who was called Laura. But I had seen her talking to Laura when we had been at the offices.

'Prince?' The white-haired lady held her bag by the handle as she asked my name, the shoulder strap falling down.

'Yeah,' I said cautiously. She sounded worried. I don't like it when adults are worried. When adults are worried you know something is up.

'Are Mr and Mrs Milandu in?'

'Er, Ruth is,' I replied. 'Hang on.' I turned into the hallway. 'Ruth,' I yelled.

I could hear Ruth moving pans in the kitchen, the crashes as she rooted around in the cupboard and the clang as she found the one she needed and put it on the stove. I shouted again.

'I'm coming, I'm coming!' she called back.

I turned back to the lady. 'She's coming,' I said.

The lady smiled at me. I didn't smile back.

'Hello.' Ruth surprised me. She walked very quietly in her fluffy slippers. She always said that she loved her home comforts.

'Hello,' the lady said, 'I'm Janice Eaton, I'm from Social Services.' As she said this, she brandished the ID card at Ruth. 'Can I come inside and talk?'

'Sure, sure,' Ruth said. I could hear the note of concern in her voice in spite of her casual response. 'Come on through to the kitchen.' She turned to me. 'Why don't you watch a bit more telly?'

I remained standing in the hall as they closed the kitchen door.

I didn't want to watch the television. I wanted to know what the lady had come to say. It was about me and Em. Something was wrong. Maybe we'd have to move again.

I stepped into the living room, then back into the hall. I hesitated there for a few minutes. Ruth's radio was now off and the pans were silent. Softly muffled voices and sound of the kettle beginning to boil drifted to me from the gap under the door.

I edged forward. Jubrel had told me, 'If the door is closed, it's closed for a reason.' But he wasn't there right then. I crept all the way up to the door and stood listening. I could just hear them over the hissing steam.

'All I can say for sure, right now, is what this woman is telling us,' the social worker said as the kettle clicked off loudly.

What woman? I thought.

'But you don't know yet?' Ruth said.

'No, we don't know, but her story seems to match the boys'.'

The boys, me and Em? My mind was whirring, my pulse racing.

They were quiet for a while after this. All I could hear was my heart-beat growing gradually louder, filling my throat and my ears.

Then Ruth broke the silence.

'Well, we won't tell Prince anything yet, but if you have found their mother . . .'

My heart beat pounded against my ribcage. I nearly threw up.

Chapter 5

Eastern Katanga, Democratic Republic of Congo, four years ago

'Go on, my little Prince!' she screamed.

It was school sports day. A good day. At my school in London, the main event was the sprint. Back home, the main event was the long-distance run. My father had pegged out the course the night before. He always came to the school and helped on sports day. I think he enjoyed it almost as much as we did.

My mother came too. 'Go on, my little Prince!' she screamed as we stood on the start line, all fourteen boys in our class, aged between five and nine. 'Go on, Emmy!' she added, the long material of her green dress billowing out behind her.

Some of the boys were much bigger than me,

even bigger than Em. But I knew I'd win that year. I had been third the year before, fifth the year before that. I knew I'd win. I had to win.

My teacher explained the course to us all again. 'You run to the end of the road,' he started, 'then left at the split tree, over to the well, left again, down the track, left at the marker, then back to here. OK?'

We all nodded. My stomach rolled inside me.

'You'll definitely win this year, Prince,' my brother whispered into my ear.

My confidence returned. 'Of course I will, slow-coach,' I replied.

'Go on, Emmy! Go on, my little Prince!' my mother screamed again. Other parents hollered for their own children, a cacophony of cheers and whoops.

My teacher gave one more instruction. 'Just follow the little flags, OK?'

We nodded for a second time.

'On your marks,' he called, 'get set . . .'

He paused and my mother screamed again, 'Go on, my boys!'

'Go!'

Everyone wanted to win and expected the elbows that pushed and bumped from left and right. The road was straight and several smaller boys sprinted ahead. They'd be worn out before they hit the tree. I kept pace with the tallest boys in the school, a few steps behind. Em was a yard or two further back. My brother would fight as hard as the others, but running wasn't really his thing. He was more of a thinker, Em.

As the dust swirled around us and the parents' cries urged us down the road, something green caught my eye. A swathe of patterned material flew towards the well. She would beat us there, I could see, and this knowledge bade me run faster.

At the tree I overtook the taller boys. They let me go, believing I'd tire before the end, and now I was fast closing in on the frontrunners. I made the left turn and saw her. My mother was jumping up and down, waving wildly, her shouts carried away by the wind. I ran even harder.

By the time I reached the well and my mother's smiling face I had outdistanced all the other runners.

'You are doing so well, my little Prince,' she said, clapping her hands and calling out to my brother.

Before I reached the final turn my lungs began to burn. Perhaps I had done too much, I thought. I could hear the thunder of feet behind me, chasing. I was certain I'd soon be caught. Then I saw her. A green beacon, waving again, her voice indistinct amongst the parents' yells. She'd run back already, she was at the finish line.

Again my feet pounded against the packed dirt. Green filled my vision. My legs were lead, my chest a furnace, my eyes swam. I kept on towards the green. I knew the other boys would be on me if I faltered even a step, but the sight of my mother dragged me onwards.

I crashed over the line into my father's arms. He lifted me straight on to my mother's shoulders. They whooped and cheered. Other parents and the taller boys slapped me on the back. Em was there too, smiling.

'Well done, my little Prince!' my mother screamed.

Chapter 6

Our mother. They'd found our mother. Our mother had found us.

I didn't hear another word after that. If my beating heart was loud before, it was nothing compared to the blood booming through my ears now. My throat tightened and my jaw clenched, reminding me of the cold earlier that afternoon.

I turned and ran down the hall, crashing past the coat-stand, my precariously balanced coat finally parachuting to the floor. As I ran up the stairs I glimpsed Ruth emerge from the kitchen, but I wasn't stopping. I hit my bedroom door at a sprint and slammed it behind me.

Had she come to find us? Did I want her to find

us? The woman who sent us away? The woman who turned me into a thief? The woman who had abandoned us to chance? Did I miss her?

'Knock, knock.' Ruth called this from behind my bedroom door, though she didn't actually knock. 'Can I come in?'

I was sprawled across my bed, so I leapt up and found myself pushing my chest of drawers in front of the door. No one was coming in.

'I just want to talk to you about what you heard, Prince.'

I didn't answer. I sat down on the floor in front of the chest, which was now blocking the door completely. I sat there for a long time.

When Ruth gave up trying to talk to me through the door, the social-worker lady tried. She didn't try for very long though. Soon I heard the front door close behind her.

Later Ruth told me that Jubrel was on his way home. Later still the phone rang, and Ruth answered it downstairs. I couldn't hear what she said.

I don't remember much more, except one thought that kept washing through my brain.

'I don't remember what she looks like.'

'I don't remember what my mother looks like.'

'I don't even remember what my own mother looks like.'

The growing darkness outside had crept into my room by the time Jubrel whispered at my closed door.

'I'm coming in, Prince,' he said. Then the door began to creep open, the heavy chest glided across the floor, pushing me ahead, like a train beginning to move, slowly but surely.

I didn't try to stop him. I got up from in front of the drawers and sat down on my bed.

When the door was open enough, Jubrel squeezed through the gap. I didn't look up at him, but I could feel his eyes on me. He came and sat down next to me, put his arm round my shoulders and waited. He still wore his suit, and his shiny shoes pointed up at me as I stared at the floor.

I didn't know what he was waiting for. There was no signal, he was silent. But as we sat there a tear bloomed in my eye, then another and another, until I could no longer blink the drops away and my yellow football shirt began to feel damp.

Why I cried, what I was feeling, I couldn't tell you.

The tears seemed to well up from some unknown place within me, from the same place where my memories were hidden.

I cried a lot and we talked a little.

They didn't know if it was really her, I found out. A lady who they thought might be our mother was waiting to meet us.

How had she found us?

He didn't know.

Was she our mother?

He didn't know.

Was everything going to be OK?

Yes, Jubrel was sure it would be.

He asked if I wanted to meet her.

Did I want to meet her?

Yes.

'When?' I asked.

'Soon. There are a few more checks they need to do, paper-work stuff,' he said. 'But soon.'

Chapter 7

Ruth and Jubrel's House, London, eight months ago

From the first night that I knew him, Jubrel understood. He always knew what to say and what not to. He was safe.

+++

'This is us.' Laura, my social worker, peered over the top of her glasses at the house in front of us.

I didn't look up but continued to stare sullenly down at my feet.

'Come on, Prince.' Laura tried to put a hand on my shoulder but I shrugged it away. 'Ruth and Jubrel are lovely, they've looked after lots of children.'

Laura pushed her glasses up her nose with her forefinger. She was always doing that. 'You should be grateful, they don't usually take . . .'

I looked up. 'What?' I said. 'They don't usually take what? Thieves?' I spat out the word, angry. I should have been nice to Laura, she was nice to me. Not everyone had been, after all that had happened, the crime, the violence, the lives we led.

'I wasn't going to say that, Prince. They don't usually take children who are so – unhappy. You are very unhappy, Prince, whether you want to admit it or not.'

Yes, I was very unhappy.

'You need someone to look after you,' Laura continued. 'I think Ruth and Jubrel are just the right people for you.'

I didn't want just the right people. I wanted my brother. Laura knew where he was, I'd asked her. But she wasn't allowed to tell me anything.

I didn't want to talk any more. Laura had tried to talk to me about my unhappiness before, it made me uncomfortable. I started walking up the five steps that I would later come to know so well, towards the house which would shortly be my home. 'Come on then,' I said, still angry.

The house was warm, I remember that from the first day. It was always warm. Ruth needed the heating on, she said. She was a tropical lady. Jubrel was always sneaking it back down but his wife was a human thermometer and within minutes she'd exclaim, 'Oh, it's getting chilly in here,' or, 'You messing with my thermostat again, you cruel man?'

The warmth went deeper than that, though. It was in Ruth's smile, in her peanut butter on toast, in her knowing looks when I told her that I had no homework. It was in Jubrel's voice, calm and measured, in his hands, laid on a shoulder, in his jokes.

But that first night I didn't want their warmth.

Laura introduced us all. 'Prince, this is Ruth and Jubrel.'

'Hello, Prince, you are so welcome,' Ruth said.

'We hear that you like football,' Jubrel said.

I said nothing.

Ruth showed me around.

'This is the lounge, we just got this new bean-bag.'

'The garden's small, but the park is just nearby.'

'So, this is your room. I really hope you'll be comfortable.'

I stared at my feet.

Then Laura said goodbye, pushing up her glasses again. 'Ruth and Jubrel are good people, Prince. Cheer up and I'm sure you'll have a great time. I will come tomorrow and take you to your new school.'

Once she'd left, with a ruffle of my hair, my new foster carers tried to talk to me. I shrugged, grunted, gave a word or two. Even then I could feel the warmth, but I was frosty. I wanted my brother, nothing but that would warm me.

Soon they gave up. 'OK, you make yourself at home.' They left me perched on the bean-bag in the lounge, my coat still on.

Twenty minutes later Jubrel came back in. He carried a wooden case about the size of a shoe box. He placed it on the floor between us as he sat.

'Can I show you something, Prince?'

The heavy box had my attention and I nodded.

As he reached forward to open the box I shifted on the bean-bag, sitting up straighter. The lid swung open and I drew breath. Nestled amongst brittle, folded paper was a gun, an ancient-looking revolver, mostly metal, a deep brown metal apart from the handle, which was wooden.

'Don't worry, it's not a working gun any more,'

Jubrel said. Then he gestured for me to pick it up.

I hesitated. I'd never held a gun. It was heavier than I'd expected. I turned it over, feeling the weight of the cold metal. Engraved in the handle was a series of numbers and two letters, E.M.

'It was my father's,' Jubrel said. 'His most prized possession.'

I had nothing to say to this but held out the gun to my new foster carer.

'He won it from an Italian army officer in the war. Maybe you'd like to hear that story one day?' He raised an eyebrow and I nodded.

Jubrel looked back down at the gun. 'He treasured this. And before he died, he gave it to me. Now it's my most prized possession. It's worth a lot of money, this chunk of metal, but I'd never sell it.' He cradled the weapon, looking down at his baby. 'My father has been gone many years, but he gave me this. That's why I treasure it. And I remember all the good things, the happiness.'

I didn't know why he was telling me this and still I had nothing to say.

'We lose people, we all lose people, sooner or later. But we still hold them, sometimes we hold them even closer. Family, the people we love, who love us, they are the best things in this world.'

Now we were getting to the crunch.

'But if we hold them too close, too tight, we have no room for anything else. No room for the rest of life.' He bent down and carefully placed the revolver back into its box. 'Think on it, Prince,' he said as he left, placing a hand on my shoulder.

I didn't shrug it away.

Chapter 8

Fresh blood is brighter than you'd think, more vivid, slick like oil, not what you'd expect. It's somehow less red too. In movies and in our minds it's scarlet like a football shirt, but it's far deeper in reality: more real.

As the blood slithered like so many snakes across the playground I knew I'd gone too far.

George knocked for me in the morning, like every other day. But that day wasn't like any other day. At least it didn't feel like it. Everything had changed – or nothing had changed. I had a mum –

or it was still just me and Em. 'Soon.' We'd know soon.

I was desperate to talk to my brother, but it had been late when I'd finished with Jubrel, too late to call. In the morning, it had been a rush; Jubrel and Alice had to get to work, I had to get to school and I was moving slower than usual. I had to wait for the end of the day when Em was picking me up.

You know when people stare at the sky and say that this cloud looks like a car and this one's like a football boot and another like a gun? George did that a lot. That morning he thought he saw the rapper Lil' Legacy's face in the clouds.

I could never see anything. George always said I needed to have more imagination. I've never been too good at imagining things. I can run faster, kick a ball harder and solve trickier maths problems than most other kids. But ask me to paint a picture and you'll have a brown blob soaking into a piece of paper; ask me to picture a scene and I'll close my eyes like the rest of them, but there's nothing there; ask me to hum a tune and one note is all you'll get. That's just the way it is.

Normally I'd laugh at George and say his clouds didn't look anything like motorbikes or fish or whatever he was chatting about. Today I didn't say anything.

'You OK?' George asked.

'Yeah,' I lied, but in my head the same thought returned. *I don't know what my mother looks like.*

It wasn't far to school, I didn't have long to think and we didn't talk about much else. When we got there, George headed to the football pitch. I told him I'd be right behind. Instead I slipped off and sat in the back playground; it was quiet there.

When the bell rang I went and lined up; I stood in the right place and waited. On an ordinary day I would have ignored the bell and been charging around until my teacher appeared. But I didn't feel like charging.

'Hey, Prince.' Matthew sidled up next to me. Everyone liked Matthew. He wasn't great at football or very smart in lessons, but he was the best at being nice.

I nodded to him in response.

'You have a good weekend?' he asked, his eternal grin doing little to change my mood.

'Yeah,' I replied, half truthfully. I did have a great time with Em but that seemed like a long time ago. So much had happened since then. A sing-song voice filled my ears as I desperately searched for a face to match.

'I went to my Nan's.' Our teacher appeared as Matthew said this. I was glad of the interruption.

All morning, my friends tried to talk to me. My teacher wanted to know what was wrong. Francesca, who is like a teacher but doesn't have a class, took me out of maths and asked me questions. I gave everyone the same response. 'I'm fine,' I said.

As the day progressed, my insides churned, a knot rose up my throat and my head pounded.

I can't tell you how I felt, because I don't really know.

At lunchtime, George cornered me. He wouldn't let up till I told him what was going on.

'My mum might be here,' I said.

'What?' Unlike most people, George knew all about us, leaving our parents, my uncle kicking us out, joining a gang, all of that. He knew I hadn't seen my mum in years. I'd told him everything.

'Really?' he continued. 'Have you seen her?' George didn't have a mum, she died a long time ago. I didn't know what was worse, knowing that your mum would never come back, like George, or not knowing anything.

'No, but we will soon.' We were in the lunch queue. We were first lunch, 'cos it was our turn on the football pitch. We talked in hushed voices, the kind you used when you didn't want the teacher to hear you. 'It might not be her.'

As I handed George his tray, I noticed a large bruise covering the back of his hand. I stared at it. George quickly put it in his pocket.

'It might not be her?' George was puzzled. 'Who else would it be?'

'I don't know.'

Abdi and Tom, boys from the other year 6 class, walked past.

'We're gonna destroy you today,' Abdi grinned.

Neither of us replied. Tom's laugh echoed in our ears as they walked to the back of the queue.

'Are you OK?'

'I don't know,' I repeated.

When we had our lunch (vegetable chilli and baked potato) slopped on our trays, George spoke again.

'Are we still playing football?'

I laughed for a moment, my mother forgotten. 'Of course we're playing and they are not gonna destroy us.'

Chapter 9

I kicked off with a pass to George, sliding the ball across the concrete to his waiting feet. I knew, even with this first pass, that something was wrong with my friend.

Normally he would have trapped the ball under the sole of his trainer, then looked up to pass again, or turned on the ball and set off dribbling, dazzling the defenders with an array of skills. Today he did neither, but threw his leg out clumsily. The ball struck his shin and rolled into the opposition's path. Tom gathered it up and ran down-pitch towards our goal. George stood glumly as I screamed at him to track back. Yeah, this was definitely not the usual George.

I chased Tom down, tackling him with the help of one of my team mates. I took the ball on, and passed to Rossella (she was a girl, but was better than most of the boys in our class). She passed back and I flicked it on to George, who was marked by Abdi. My friend didn't move and Abdi darted in front of him, stealing the ball from under his nose. Again we chased the attackers back towards our goal.

We followed their passes, doing our best to mark them, Abdi, Tom, Lee, Shakur, back to Tom. The ball at his feet, Tom struck it forcefully. It sailed through the air, goal-bound.

We had a good keeper. He leapt and got a hand to the ball, which fell to George, who was waiting stiffly on the edge of the penalty box. He kicked it away, not the confident clearance of a quality footballer, but a flailing whack, desperate to be rid of the ball.

What had happened to my best friend?

It may seem a small thing, but George's football skills were one of the certainties in my life. Was everything changing, was everything falling apart?

The game went on and George's feet did not improve, no matter how much we shouted at him. If anything, the shouting made him worse. His head dropped and he barely touched the ball before one of the opposition snatched it away. I could see he was trying, but there was no skill left in his feet. Despite the rising anger and panic, I tried to stop shouting at him.

Was I angry with George? Not really. But the people I wanted to shout at, my mum, my dad, even Em, weren't there. And suddenly, victory seemed vital to me. If we lost, someone would pay.

Even without George's usual skills, we could still have beaten them. I was still the best player on the pitch and the rest of the team could play. We even scored the first goal, Rossella scrambling it in at the near post from a corner kick. But we couldn't hold them back for long and my belief in our chances began to disappear when they equalised a few minutes later, quickly followed by a second. A third, five minutes after that, killed all hope of us succeeding.

For the rest of the game I couldn't look up without one of the opposition smirking at me. I thought my eyes would be dry forever after the tears of the night before, but I was wrong. A drop ran down my cheek.

'Ah, is the baby losing?' Lee said, as Abdi laughed wickedly behind him. My anger began to reach new heights at every comment.

Tom kept winking at me. 'Better luck next time,

eh?' he called as he watched their fourth goal sail past our keeper.

One final goal, from me this time, did nothing in the end. I hammered it into the net, relieving only a small fraction of my anger. We still lost miserably.

'Four-Two, Four-Two, Four-Two . . .'

The chants began as we headed towards the water fountains. George disappeared. Maybe he was worried we'd be angry, I think some of the team were. I definitely was, kicking at the wall as the rest of the team trotted behind, surrounded by the gleeful shouts of the other class.

Abdi broke off from the chanting and threw his arm around my shoulders. 'Ah, little Princey,' he said in a whining baby voice, 'did you lose the football game?'

I didn't answer. The rage was now swelling inside me, choking all other thoughts. I looked around, challenging.

'Ah! Is the baby upset?' Shakur pouted as he said this, looking at me with his big eyes. I wanted to claw them out.

'Ah, little Princey,' Tom echoed, then turned and chuckled to his friends.

I'd had enough. I rushed forward and pushed

Tom with all the force I had.

He crashed into the wall, his head connecting with a short black pipe that jutted out of the brickwork. 'Ah!' He let out a scream – not a shout of anger, but an involuntary yelp.

We all stopped and watched as Tom clutched at his head. He brought his hands away, covered in deep red blood. Then he collapsed forward, his bloodied hands groping at my white T-shirt.

Then the blood came.

Kids poured in from around the playground whilst the blood poured from the boy's wound and teachers called for everyone to 'Get Back!' and 'Line up!'

Fresh blood is brighter than you'd think, more vivid, slick like oil, not what you'd expect. It's somehow less red too. In movies and in our minds it's scarlet like a football shirt, but it's far deeper in reality: more real.

As the blood slithered like so many snakes across the playground, I knew I'd gone too far.

Anger fled, replaced by blind panic.

Chapter 10

Ilala Market, Dar Es Salaam, Tanzania

If he saw a sleek black car or large men in suits, Céléstin would pack up quickly and leave his broken table to clatter to the floor. Other stall-holders would curse him, and his whispered apologies and bowed head did little to stem their anger as he crashed past their stalls.

The debt was more than he could hope to pay back. Céléstin had borrowed a lot. Just enough for one plane ticket out of the city.

Most days the gangsters came calling, seeking some repayment. Céléstin had little to offer them and the threats had turned to violence. So, if he saw the car or the suits, my father fled.

Desperately he sought other work, but he had no success. He thought about running further away than the other side of the market – out of the city and away. But he daren't. The gangsters knew who'd taken that plane ticket and where they'd gone. Céléstin didn't know if they could reach her there – but he would not risk it. So he stayed, but he kept out of their way as much as possible.

The morning had gone well. He'd traded with Godwin, and had some jewellery to sell. Céléstin suspected his friend had been too generous, but he was in no position to shun charity. His cough hadn't been so bad either.

With the jewellery sold and some notes rolled up in his Kanzu, the afternoon dragged on. As the market emptied, Godwin came over as usual, bringing a cup of strong, bitter tea.

'Did you watch the match, my friend?' he asked. Football frenzy filled the city. Tanzania's Taifa Stars versus Ghana's Black Stars had been on everyone's lips. It was an important match – the winners would go to the World Cup. 'If I see that Juma Kwame

I'll lynch him,' Godwin continued.

Céléstin nodded in reply. He'd heard similar threats all morning and most were a lot stronger than his friend's. Until yesterday Juma Kwame, Tanzania's captain, had been a star, celebrated around the world and worshipped at home. Now he was the villain in the biggest drama in the country's biggest sport.

Céléstin hadn't seen the match but he knew, like everyone else in Dar Es Salaam's streets, that Kwame had given away a penalty which had sealed the Taifa Stars' fate: another World Cup that Tanzania would not play in.

Godwin prattled on. Football, family, money, his usual subjects filled the conversation. Céléstin nodded, laughed, sipped at his tea, whilst keeping watch.

The car was not the one he was used to, but he recognised the first face that peered out of the window. He thrust the tea-cup at his friend, who had come to expect this kind of behaviour.

Godwin looked over his shoulder. 'Three of them,' he said. 'A new one, I think. Big man, really big man.'

Godwin's comments didn't help Céléstin's packing, neither did a fresh fit of coughing.

He dragged his remaining stock (some clothing, a few books, a cracked picture frame) into the battered suitcase. He made ready to run. One final look to see his debt collectors approaching. Then he stopped, suitcase in hand, his breath stilled.

'Why aren't you running?' Godwin muttered through gritted teeth.

'I know that man. The new one, the big one, I know him.'

Godwin looked back over his shoulder at the big man in question. He strode behind the other two, dark glasses shielding his eyes.

'Who is he?' my father's friend asked.

'That is my brother. That's Victor.'

Chapter 11

Tom was not in too bad a state, despite the gushing blood. They thought he just had a bad cut and had been knocked out by the collision with the wall. An ambulance came, patched him up and took him away. He was grinning as they loaded him into the back of the white van; he was meant to be having a reading test that afternoon.

I had a clear view of all of this through the window in the head-teacher's office. 'You'll need to wait here till your parents come to get you,' the secretary said.

I didn't bother to correct her. She couldn't get hold of Ruth or Jubrel. I knew she wouldn't, they'd be working.

'Maybe you could phone my brother, Mrs Boyes?'
I suggested.

The head-teacher gave me her most fearsome look
again. She'd been directing it at me for the last two
hours as I sat in her office, being shouted at by her,
Miss Strong, my teacher, and Mr Alan, who was in
charge of Year Five and Year Six.

I knew I'd done the wrong thing. I'd said sorry. I
had nothing else to say. When Mrs Boyes suggested
that they might need to call the police to 'have a little
talk with me', I nearly cracked. My voice went all
high and a tear formed in the corner of my eye. That
seemed to calm them down a bit.

'Maybe that won't be necessary,' said Mr Alan,
'but you've got to think about where you're heading,
Prince.'

Where was I heading? Was there a new home for
me? Would we be a family again? What was at the
end of this unknown road?

Em didn't even look in my direction when he
came to collect me from the stuffy office. I'd seen him
this angry before. But along with the anger was fear,
sadness, panic. He looked how I felt.

Mrs Boyes let me go with my brother, vowing
that she was going to get hold of my carers before

the evening was out.

'What the hell, Prince?' We'd walked a few metres from the school gate when Em started shouting. 'What are you doing? Do you think I know how to deal with this either?'

I didn't know what to say to that. I replied simply and quietly. 'Sorry.'

'Who do you really want to hit, Prince? None of us know what to do.' Em was still shouting and I could feel my anger rising too. 'If she's here, she's here, and we'll deal with it. I don't need you doing, doing – this!'

I was at breaking point now. I stopped, and turned to face my brother. We glared into each other's eyes.

'Shut up,' I hissed. 'I've had enough of not having anyone and not knowing anything. I've had enough!' My voice had been getting louder as I spoke and I was gasping as I finished the sentence.

'What do you mean, not having anyone? You've got me, Prince.' Em's anger began to melt, he was almost pleading.

Our fury melted, replaced by fear. What our future held was clear to neither of us.

'Come on.' Our argument was over, Em beckoned for me to follow.

But the fear was too great for me. Maybe Em could walk towards the unknown mother, the stranger who we hadn't seen for oh so long, but I couldn't.

I ran.

Chapter 12

I ran, unthinking, down one street, round a corner, along another. Shops, houses, a school flitted by. My feet pounded the pavement. Some roads I knew, others I did not. They blurred together in the tears that glazed my eyes. I careered into people, who called after me: I did not look back. When I collided with a car door that opened as I passed, I stumbled but continued.

If, in that mad rush, you'd stopped me and asked me why I was running, I don't think I could have answered you. I was not thinking. I was running from thought.

If you ask me now, I'm still not entirely sure.

This I do know, it was all too much, change after change, hope, disappointment, fear. I'd had enough.

I wanted to be happy, but that seemed out of reach, unattainable. No matter how good Jubrel and Ruth were to me, they were not my family. But who were my family? I only knew my brother. Who was this woman who'd come for us?

In my memories of her, the tiny morsels that remained, my mother was full of happiness, smiling, singing, my father laughing in the background. But my fears, awash with panic, loomed much larger in my mind.

Like I said, I'm not entirely sure why I ran.

It must have been only a few minutes later when I stopped, doubled over and retched, but it seemed like hours. My stomach turned itself inside out and I spat the bile onto the floor. My lungs burned and my legs had turned to blocks of wood, heavy and rigid. Bent over, still retching, my head began to swim. I straightened up and tried to stop myself collapsing. I shook my head. The swimming stopped, replaced by a dull throb.

A bus-stop was the only landmark by which to find my bearings. Otherwise, all I could see were characterless houses, lamp-posts alight in the evening gloom, and rows of parked cars. I walked slowly in case the faintness returned, to the bus-stop.

Leaning against the post, the throbbing began to lessen. Thoughts about what I was doing, where I was going and why, floated just beyond the pain of my head, legs, lungs and the emptiness of my stomach.

When a bus came along, I got on.

I pulled my jacket close and sat as far from the other passengers as possible, scrunched into a corner, on the back seat.

As I watched the world outside, my pains began to disappear and thoughts crowded my head. I let my mind wander back to my brother. He'd have called Alice by now and tried to get hold of Ruth and Jubrel. They'd tell him to come home, that I'd be back soon enough. But I knew what he would do. Emmanuel would always come for me.

I played out his search in my head until the bus driver called, 'Last stop.'

I got off the bus and, surprisingly, I knew where I was. A vast building stretched into the sky in front of me. The last stop was the first place Em and I had seen in London. When we had run from my uncle Victor, we had set off on a journey that ended at this same train station.

I entered the building and decided to stay there, sitting on a metal seat, before curling up in a quiet corner whilst the station emptied of the last few commuters. Then I slept.

Chapter 13

**Eastern Katanga, Democratic Republic
of Congo, four years ago**

I had slept outside once before, back in Africa, with
the stars above me and the moon looking down. I'd
enjoyed it that time.

We celebrated my sports-day victory with a
feast. I can't remember my mother's face, but I can
remember what we ate on that warm evening: peanut
and chicken soup, greens and beans, and a kind of
mash stuff which my mum called Fufu and my dad
called something that I don't know how to write. I
guess the food was easy to remember because Ruth
made some of the same things, so I still saw them.
But I hadn't seen my mother's face, not even a photo,
in four years.

After we'd filled our stomachs, Em went to fetch water for the morning. He had been doing it on his own the past few weeks. I didn't envy him – it was a hard job, dark too, just the moon to light his way back.

My jobs were much easier. I cleared away the bowls, taking them to my mother, who washed them whilst she hummed a soft tune. Then she took the eating mat outside and shook off any crumbs. I hung up one mat and got out our four sleeping mats.

With our jobs done, me and Em lay down. I could not sleep though, adrenalin rushed through me, with visions of billowing green. My legs continued to pump and my ears rang with the raised voices. I lay, my eyes still open.

Eventually I got up and crept outside, where I knew my parents would be sitting. As I reached the door I could hear muffled laughter, two deep snorts.

My mother's low voice said, 'Shh, don't wake the boys.'

Outside I found my uncle Victor, his hand on my dad's shoulder. All three were sitting on makeshift chairs of upturned pans.

'Mum,' I said. 'I can't sleep.'

'See what you've done,' she said, pretending to

glare at my father and uncle. 'Come here, Princey,' she said to me.

'The little champion.' My uncle grinned. 'I've been hearing all about it.' I smiled in return. 'You know I was a runner once too?'

I shook my head.

'I was a champ like you.' I reached my mother's arms as Victor said this, and she folded them around me.

'Here, my Prince,' said my father. 'Victor brought you this.' He held out a brown paper bag. I knew exactly what was inside, nuts and sweets. Victor lived in town and, on special occasions, this is what he brought us.

'Say thank you,' my mother whispered.

'Thank you, Uncle,' I beamed.

He beamed right back.

My father fetched the sleeping mats and we lay down right there.

'The fresh air will put you to sleep,' my mother said. And she was right. With my father, mother and Uncle Victor whispering around me I drifted off.

Later, I came to know a very different Victor. He became a figure of nightmares, his face etched with anger. Many times I wished I could have my other uncle back, the one who brought me gifts, whose laughter filled a room. But he was gone, replaced by a looming shadow of violence that haunted my dreams.

Chapter 14

'Lightning?' I woke up to the sound of a familiar voice, not my brother's though.

'It is him.' Another familiar voice. I stretched, began to open my eyes and felt the aches and bruises that come from a night on a cold hard floor.

Two faces, one dark as strong tea, the other like a clock face, white with contrasting black features, swam into my blurry morning vision. Two faces I did not expect to see. Two faces from my past.

'Morning, Princey,' the Asian boy squeaked, his childish voice matching his height.

I just gawped at the two of them.

'Have you gone a bit special in the head or

something?' As he said this, the white boy stretched out his long leg and poked me with the end of his crisp white trainer.

'Ibby? Kieran?' I couldn't believe it.

'All right, Lightning?' Ibby nodded this reply whilst Kieran looked over his shoulder. Then the taller boy pulled out a packet of cigarettes and offered one to Ibby, who shook his head. I said no too.

Once upon a time I had seen these boys as family. Well, the only family I had at least. We had run around the streets of London together, stealing what we could. We'd had money then, big houses to live in, food whenever we wanted. None of it was ours, of course. I thought I'd been happy. I thought I was looked after, safe.

'What you doing here?' Kieran asked between puffs. 'You look a mess.'

'Yeah, you do look a state, man,' Ibby chipped in.

I looked down at myself. Tom's blood was still splattered across my shirt.

'I'm . . .' I didn't know what to say. *I'm running away from… from… what?* I did not know. *I've turned my back on something that you two would kill for, a real family, somewhere to call home. I'm running away from the best thing I could have.*

Ibby didn't wait for me to finish my sentence. 'I thought you'd do better than this, man.' The two boys sat down beside me on the cold marble floor. 'You were always the best.'

I knew what he was talking about. I could steal anything in those days. Nothing stopped me, Lightning Fingers.

'No, I'm not . . .' Another sentence I didn't know how to complete, so I looked around the station, the blur of sleep blinked from my eyes.

Business people, their suits crisp and their hair slick, tourists, some with luggage bigger than themselves, and men in yellow jackets and uniforms, milled about. Some, mostly the tourists, stood and watched the giant board, waiting for their train. Others, the suits this time, crowded the coffee stands. The train workers, their sullen faces discouraging conversation from customers, stood in little knots near the barriers that separated our part of the station from the platforms.

'We got our own crew now, Lightning.' Ibby filled the silence I left again. 'Haven't we, Kier?'

Kieran nodded sagely, taking a last pull on the poisonous stick. He flicked it on to the station floor and crushed it under his foot before he spoke.

'We could use you though, Lightning. Some of these guys we've got are a bit . . .' He shrugged to complete his sentence.

'Yeah, you should join us. We'd let you in at the top, of course, get a cut of the best, like us,' Ibby said.

I looked them up and down. From their white-clad feet to their black-capped crowns, they were wearing some of the sharpest clothes a boy like me could wish for. Wasn't this what I wanted? Money, clothes, luxury, the best things in life?

Money equals happiness, I thought.

'I don't know,' I said aloud.

'We'd better get on,' Kieran said. He was gruffer than I remembered. In my memory he was always quick with a joke, a grin or a laugh.

'Yeah, yeah,' Ibby replied. Then, to me he said, 'We'll be around, hitting the station today, so, if you change your mind . . .' Ibby rubbed his fingers and thumb together. Money.

I watched them walk away as my brother had watched me run a few hours before.

What did I want? Was I watching it in the reflected brilliance of bright white trainers and the quick glances from side to side to look for the next target, the next pay packet? Or had I run from it?

+++

I sat thinking for a long time, on the same piece of cold floor. My rumbling stomach didn't shift me, nor did the numbness spreading up my back. Eventually one of the yellow jackets asked me to move as he swept up discarded cardboard coffee cups, free newspapers and Kieran's cigarette butt.

The morning rush ended, and now the crowds were just tourists and late office workers, rushing past the Asian men positioned throughout the station, handing out free newspapers. I found an empty bench; I didn't want to sit next to anyone. I swept a leaflet off my perch after reading its slogan.

'Is there more to life than this?' the leaflet asked.

Time passed. I thought about money, about family, about what I really wanted. The station began to fill with a lunchtime rush, and people crowded the coffee stands again. I spotted Ibby and Kieran as they stalked a group of tourists loaded down with cameras and bags. I kept them in sight and in mind.

When I heard footsteps approaching my bench I didn't look up. I realised tears had filled my eyes. I scrubbed them away as the footsteps stopped beside me.

A gentle hand was placed on my shoulder and the most familiar voice of all whispered, 'Prince.'

I looked up through freshly blooming tears into my brother's face. Neither of us spoke as he sat down beside me. I knew all along that Em would find me here. I guess I wanted him to.

'She is back,' Em said. 'It is our mother.'

The silence hung heavy again.

'Prince?'

A sing-song voice filled my mind and a rich, deep laugh.

A real voice said again, 'Prince?'

She really is back, I thought. My hope, my anger, my dreams fought inside me. I looked at my brother, his face a picture of reassurance. I looked at Ibby and Kieran, approaching the wealthy tourists. I saw what they'd probably take, a handbag perched on top of a wheelie-suitcase. What did I want?

'Come on, Prince.' Em stood up, beckoning me.

I stood slowly and my brother waited. I glanced over at the two pickpockets again, their expensive street clothes looking out of place amongst the throng of tourists in checked shirts and hiking boots. I looked back at my brother, his old scuffed trainers, the jeans with a gaping hole in the knee, his faded football shirt, and a face I knew better than my own.

What did I want?

I took one step, and another.

Then I walked out of the station, my brother's arm round me. I didn't look back.

Chapter 15

Heathrow Airport, London,
three weeks earlier

The flight had taken close to ten hours but it seemed to Remi that her tears had not stopped flowing for even a minute. She flew into the unknown, to a land she'd never seen and a future she could not predict.

In her mind she saw her husband's face, smiling through his own tears, waving. She saw him in the city she had left. She saw him but did not know if she would ever see him again.

She saw her sons too, her little boys, the boys she'd cherished, then sent out into the unknown. Remi tried to picture them, boys grown.

All she wanted was her family. She had little left

but her hopes. She hoped she flew toward them. She hoped that Victor had kept them safe. She hoped she'd find them soon and they'd banish the emptiness she felt, the gaping hole left by the farewell to her husband.

When she touched down in England and emerged from the sprawling airport, the sun broke through the white clouds, ushering in a patch of blue. Remi took this as a sign. She would do all she could to find her boys and usher in her own clear blue sky.

Chapter 16

When my brother found me, he took me straight back to Ruth and Jubrel. We talked on the way about the usual things, football, money – and then we talked about our mother. When he left he told me the same as Jubrel. 'We'll see her soon.'

Now, 'soon' had arrived.

'What do we do, Em?' This was the first thing I asked my brother when I saw him. He looked at me, didn't answer but grabbed me in a hug.

I had arrived at Em's house moments before,

dragging my feet behind Jubrel.

What did I expect my brother to say? We were already doing the only thing we could do. We were meeting this woman, our mother, or a stranger, or perhaps one and the same.

'Come on, Prince.' Em beckoned me through to Alice's kitchen.

Jubrel followed. 'Had a good day, Emmanuel?' he asked.

Em pushed the door open and the smell of baking wafted towards us. He replied with a shrug and the words, 'It was all right.' It seemed to me that my brother's day had been like mine, awash with uncertainty.

The moment I stepped into the kitchen Alice embraced me with warmth. She looked up from the oven, shot a beaming smile at me and bounced across the floor. 'There you are, Princey,' she said.

I didn't reply, standing stiff and still as she hugged me. My smooth dark skin and tight black hair pressed against her rough, wrinkled neck that had the feel of scrunched-up packing paper.

Alice served us biscuits and squash as we sat round the kitchen table, and both the foster carers asked us more questions about our day.

What did we learn?

Nothing.

Did I play football?

I still wasn't allowed because of 'the incident'.

How was George?

Not himself.

I knew that they were trying to help, keeping our minds off the impending meeting, but all I wanted to do was talk to my brother. Alice and Jubrel weren't the only ones making this difficult though. Em avoided my eye. Maybe he was as unsure as me. Were his memories of our mother as distant as mine? Did he know what she looked like any better than me?

The minutes stretched on like hours. The ticking of the clock grew louder. Finally, the door-bell rang. My heart leapt into my throat and my legs turned to jelly.

Alice looked at us both, took another sip of her tea, then rose slowly from her seat.

'OK, boys?' she asked.

Now Em looked me in the eye. We both nodded. Ready or not, it was time.

We heard Alice clip-clop along the hallway; we heard the heavy door creak open, coats being removed, and finally the approaching footsteps.

We watched as the kitchen door swung silently inwards. Three faces stared back at us: Ruth's, a worried crease across her forehead; the social worker's, surrounded by her halo of white hair; and a dark face, somehow, in spite of all my fears, as familiar to me as the feel of a football or the taste of peanut butter. It was my mother. It was our mother. She was back.

All confusion, all worry melted away and I leapt from my stool and raced across the room. Then Alice and the social worker moved to one side as a little cry alerted us to another presence in the room. That familiar face looked down at a bundle hung across her body.

I reached my mother, hugged her tightly and looked down at the bundle myself. My mum kissed the top of my head. I could feel her hot tears dropping down through my short hair.

'My boys,' she whispered.

Em was there beside me, looking up at our long-lost parent.

Finally my mother introduced the bundle – our sister, Grace.

Chapter 17

Some things change slowly, like the seasons; it wasn't going to be spring for at least another month. Others change in the blink of an eye, like a light suddenly coming on.

At first, my mother's arrival into our lives was like the switching on of a light. Everything changed in an instant. I said goodbye to Ruth and Jubrel.

'We're still here for you, Prince,' Jubrel said. 'If there's anything we can do to help....''

We moved, me and Emmanuel. Not far, we didn't change schools or anything, but we moved in with Mum and Grace. Emmanuel and I lived together again. We lived with our mother and we had a sister.

Other things, more important than the building you call home and the faces that fill your day, took longer to change.

We had to get to know our mum. Not many people have to do that.

She was a woman who we knew like the back of our hand, but somehow, in ways that we could not put our finger on, things had changed. She was part of us, but apart from us; we'd lived separate lives. Em, I and our mother had seen things we didn't want to see again, and been to places we didn't want to go.

She was our mum but she was a stranger.

Her face was burdened with grief and hardship which had not been there before, and behind her eyes, which had always been alight with song, was sorrow.

We held out on telling her everything. I don't know why. She knew some of it already from the social workers. Emmanuel said she wouldn't want to hear about all of that, all the theft, the violence, the lives we'd led.

She didn't tell us everything, either. When we asked where our dad was, her mouth opened and closed like a landed fish, and her eyes began to fill with tears. 'I don't know,' was all she'd say.

I believed her, but all the same I wanted to know what had happened, why our father wasn't there too.

'Stop asking Mum about him,' Emmanuel said to me one evening after we'd been living with our mother for a few days. 'Can't you see it upsets her?'

I thought about this for a moment, picking at the bobbled sheet that covered my bed: the top bunk of two.

'But where is he, Em? Is he coming?'

I heard Em roll over, on his bunk below me, before he replied. 'If Mum knew, she'd tell us.'

I had my legs in the air, walking my feet along the low ceiling. My bare feet looked almost black against the yellowed, peeling paint.

'Would she?' I sulked aloud.

Emmanuel didn't answer me for a long time. He was always the thoughtful one.

I jumped off the top bunk, a skill I had perfected on our first night in the small flat we all shared, and picked up my reading book. Everyone in my class had to take a book home. We were meant to read them, but if we just wrote in our reading journals we didn't get in trouble; that was what my teacher checked.

I plucked the book off the floor. My brother had his back to me and didn't look round as I hauled myself back up. I settled down to flick through a book about Japanese monsters and stuff. George had said it was really good and the cover wasn't boring, so I gave it a go.

'Do you remember Bigger?' Em startled me when he suddenly spoke.

'Bigger?' I had vague recollections of a smile, of sweets and laughter, a feeling of kindness, but I wasn't sure.

'He was one of our neighbours, back home.'

'Old man?' I asked as I put my finger in the page I was reading. I didn't want to lose my place. George was right, it was good.

'Yeah.' I heard Em moving again. I thought he was probably sitting up. 'He was nice, right?' I made a noise of agreement to my brother's question. 'And he was happy, yeah?' I agreed again. 'Did our father ever tell you what happened to his family?'

'Erm . . . I don't think so,' I replied, staring upwards.

'They were killed,' Em told me bluntly, 'in a war. All of them, his wife and his mum, and his kids. Even though he lost the best things in his life, he tried to carry on, carry on being happy, carry on being nice.'

My brother stopped speaking and moved again, I could hear his covers being pulled up around him. I still had my feet against the ceiling in the dark, my reading book discarded now while I thought about what my brother had said.

Before sleep overcame us both, Em had one final thing to say. 'Try to be happy, Prince.'

Chapter 18

Ruth and Jubrel's House, London, 6 months ago

You shouldn't have to try to be happy, should you? It's not something that needs work. It's something that comes to you, without effort. Isn't it?

I remember the last time that I felt happy, truly happy, where nothing else, not your problems or your worries, not your loss or regret, not your fear or your pain are remembered. It was fantastic.

I'd lived with Ruth and Jubrel for two months and I'd thought about what Jubrel had said to me. I'd tried to let go a little, to move on. I'd even started smiling, sometimes laughing.

Laura had said I could write to Em, she'd even deliver it for me.

After a lot of persuasion she had even explained to me why we weren't allowed to meet up, yet. She said people were worried about our influence on one another.

I tried to explain that Em had never been a bad influence, it was the others.

Laura said that she knew this. She was doing all she could to 'make a meeting happen'.

So, the happiness was building up. Then Jubrel announced that we were going on holiday.

Holiday! Me on holiday! Some of you will be shocked, but I'd never been on holiday, never. Well, Em told me that we'd gone to stay at a big lake when I was little, at our mother's cousins or something. But it didn't count if you couldn't remember it, did it?

'La Pignon,' Jubrel said. 'It's a campsite, in France, by the sea.'

I had no words. It was too exciting.

When the day came, we packed up Jubrel's car. Ruth stashed a large quantity of sweets in the glove compartment.

'You can't go on a long journey without them,' she said.

We were ready. I sat in the back surrounded by luggage, bags, food, camping gear. Jubrel began to pull away, then Ruth screamed, 'Stop!'

Jubrel hit the brakes and a sleeping bag slid off of the pile on to my head. 'What is it, you mad woman?' Jubrel said, and I laughed.

'Did you pack the passports?'

Jubrel pulled a face and looked back at me. 'Oops,' he said.

Ruth turned round too. 'Prince, be a darling and go get them. They're in the filing cabinet, in the study. Yours is a kind of temporary one, folded inside mine.'

Jubrel's study was the tiniest little room you could imagine, crammed with a minute desk, shelves and a filing cabinet that protruded out into the room. I knew that the locked cabinet was where Jubrel kept his father's gun too. I'd asked to see it once more.

'The code,' Ruth continued, 'is 1, 1, 2, 0. Got it?'

I nodded, smiling.

This was my happiest moment of the holiday, not the ball games in the swimming pool, not the staying up late, or being allowed to drink a shandy with my meals. It was this moment, the moment I was trusted.

Happiness came to me then.

Chapter 19

For most boys, your mum taking you shopping can be embarrassing, right? She makes you try on dead clothes. You have to go into shops that are just for ladies. And you don't even want to think about what would happen if you ran into your mates. Then you'd really be in trouble.

I should have been ecstatic to go shopping with my mum though; after all, she hadn't taken me out for years, this woman who looked and sounded so familiar, whose presence had dragged up memories lost to that hidden corner of my mind, who despite this was still a stranger. A stranger I was desperate to get to know.

And it happened this way. I couldn't wait to spend the day with her, but by the end I just wanted to disappear, to be anywhere else except shopping with my mum.

It was our first Saturday morning back together. Em had a mountain of homework so he stayed at home. If he had come it might not have been so bad.

We needed some new clothes for Grace, some food, and trainers for me. Mine had reached the end of their lives weeks ago, needing to be resuscitated every morning.

I carried her black-and-brown trolley down the stairs, three flights, then on to the street. She had Grace in a long, patterned sling. My sister was asleep. She slept a lot. Is that usual for babies?

'Thank you, Prince,' my mum said.

I smiled in reply.

We walked to the high street. My mum said we could get the bus back – she checked her purse as she said this, and then put it back into the folds of her traditional dress. I knew money was tight: the flat was sparse, the furniture threadbare and my stomach rumbled, like it hadn't done in all the months that I lived with Ruth and Jubrel. But it was a mission to the high street.

My mother asked me lots about school as we walked, my friends, my teachers, and the things I was good at.

'You were always good at sports, Prince,' she replied with a laugh.

She kept singing snatches of songs. I didn't know what to think of this. It was nice to hear her happy, and her voice teased out snippets of memory, each bringing a new smile to my face. People did give us strange looks though. Grace slept the whole way, strapped across my mum, along the main road, under the railway bridge, past the tube station.

When we finally arrived I showed Mum, through the bustle of people, the shop where Ruth had bought my last pair of trainers. I thought they had been cheap, but just about passable as cool. Ruth had said they were 'smart enough'.

We looked in at row upon row of gleaming shoes.

'Come on,' I said, then pulled my mum inside.

As soon as we passed the security barriers, I knew what I wanted. Sparkling white, big green laces and a fluorescent tick, glimmered at me from across the shop.

'These are well nice, Mum,' I said, pointing them out. I said this quietly, we weren't the only customers.

A group of boys were trying on caps, further into the shop, by the counter. Cool-looking boys, a few years older than me, they all had the best trainers money could buy.

'Hmm.' She made a noise, which didn't mean anything to me. Then she went over and picked them up.

'What?' She said this loudly, and several of the boys looked over. 'They cost how much?' She let out a big snort. I wasn't getting those trainers, that was clear.

As I tried to look cool, in spite of the trolley I was still pulling, my mum turned and glared around the shop. She walked to another shelf and picked up a disgusting shoe.

This was too much. 'No, Mum,' I hissed.

'Excuse me.' She still refused to talk quietly, or even at a normal volume. She shouted, 'You do not say no to me, young man.' I didn't know why her mood had changed so quickly. What had upset her? She stared at me hard, then glanced at the price. 'No, these are no good,' she called out. Grace let out a small whimper from within her sling. I let out a sigh.

I could hear the gang with the caps laughing, but I couldn't even glance at them. I tried to hide myself behind the rack of 'sale' shoes my mum was looking at.

She picked up several more, declaring they were no good as soon as she looked at the price.

'There is nothing here,' she finally stated as a shop assistant approached us.

'Can I help you at all?' the lady asked.

My mother smiled at her and said, 'No, thank you very much.' Then we left.

'Why did you take us in there, Prince? That was no good,' was the first thing she said to me when we got outside.

I shrugged, then neither of us spoke. I felt a bit sick. I had never been that embarrassed.

We ended up buying everything from the market. Lengths of cloth to make Grace some clothes, blue plastic bags of vegetables and a small piece of meat, and the ugliest, most clumpy, malformed, black school shoes that I had ever seen. How could I wear those monstrosities to school? I would get laughed out of the playground. My embarrassment was reaching new heights.

We did get the bus home, but we didn't talk like we had on the way out. I lugged the trolley on board while my mum paid the driver. She sat down in a seat right at the front. Grace had started to stir, so Mum began to unravel her from the sling and motioned for me to find a seat further back.

I did as I was told; I didn't really want to sit next to her anyway. But after a few minutes I realised I had sat down next to the wrong person - you know, the person on the bus who talks to themselves. The person that no one looks at, that you try to forget exists, the one who occasionally calls out to apparently imaginary people.

In this instance it was a very small, old, white lady. She wore a woollen hat and she seemed to be muttering numbers to herself as she tapped her palm with her index finger.

I looked over at my mother. I could see that she was singing under her breath as she fed Grace. How do people see my mum? I wondered. Was she the person you didn't dare look at, or the lady that the groups of teenagers sniggered at?

I realised that I did not know this woman I called Mum. I did not know what she had gone through. I did not know why she had changed so much from the singing voice in my memories.

We were strangers.

Chapter 20

I needed to talk to my brother, but Emmanuel's work kept him busy all evening. I awoke the next morning looking forward, even more than usual, to Sunday-morning football.

We snuck out as soon as we were up. My mum was awake, we could hear her talking to Grace, but we didn't disturb her. The evening before, she had agreed to let us go out as early as we liked.

The street lights still shone through a light mist, almost rain. If we had left any earlier, it would have been too dark for football.

I liked playing when it was wet. Emmanuel didn't.

'Oh,' he groaned when we got out of the flats and were presented with the weather. 'Do we have to?'

'Come on, Em. It's Sunday-morning football.' I was really excited. For the first time I didn't have to wait for Em's foster carer to bring him round. I had practically dragged my brother out of bed, thrown his football stuff at him until he'd dressed, and pushed him out of the door. 'We've gotta try out this new park,' I pleaded.

We were still standing by the flats. I knew I hadn't persuaded Emmanuel yet.

'Couldn't we just wait till it's properly light? And a bit warmer?' He zipped his coat up as he said this.

'It's not just the football. I want to talk to you, too.'

My big brother looked at me. 'Come on then.'

I grinned as we moved off down the road, heading for the football pitch.

'So, what's up, Prince?' Emmanuel asked.

'Erm.' I'd been longing to have this conversation, but now I was at a loss as to what to say. 'Mum, I guess.' It wasn't far to the park, I could see the trees in the distance and bounced the football in anticipation.

'What you on about?' my brother replied.

I thought again about how to say it, but hadn't

figured it out when my mouth started moving. 'Have you seen the shoes? It's embarrassing . . . we can't . . . we don't even have a telly . . . what are we supposed to do?'

I knew that I wasn't making sense, but I also knew that my brother understood. He knew it wasn't about the shoes or even the television.

He sighed loudly, then snatched the ball off me and bounced it himself. We could see the tall park gates now.

'They're just things, Prince. Are you even trying to just Be Happy?'

'But, but, how can I be happy when . . . when . . ?' I didn't need to finish the sentence. Em knew that our mother was not the mother we remembered. Her sadness went too deep. Silence stretched between us as the park got closer.

'What can we do?' Em shrugged.

I thought it was my brother's job to come up with the ideas but I didn't mind, 'cos I had my own idea.

'Money equals happiness.' My mantra came so easily. 'Maybe if we make some money, buy some nicer stuff, Mum will be happier.'

Em sighed and shook his head.

'Come on Em, she needs to be happy. We need her

to be happy. You're the one who keeps saying 'Try to be happy.' I'm trying, this is my way of trying. But I need you.'

'OK, OK.' Em laughed. 'I'll help.'

'What?' I asked.

'I'll help. You think money's gonna make everything better, right?'

'Er.' I thought about this again. My brother's quick agreement had thrown me. 'Yeah, I think so.'

'So, I'll help you make some money. And then we'll see if you're right.'

We entered the empty park, and a tingle went up my spine, seeing the astro-turf pitch stretched out in front of us. I knew Em wasn't really agreeing with me, he wanted to show me I was wrong. But I'd take this as far as he'd let me.

'OK. How?' I asked, grinning.

'We could . . . sell stuff.'

I looked at him blankly. What did we have to sell? In my mind I scanned the mess of our room. Really, who would buy any of that stuff? As I snatched the ball back and kicked it out ahead of us, I considered this. I took off at a run, reached the ball, turned quickly and sent the white globe spinning back towards my brother.

We played. And we talked all the while about how we could possibly make money. What did we have? What could we make? What could we do?

After an hour or so we sat by one of the goals, our legs tired. By this time the park was filling up. Some boys about my age were playing headers and volleys in the other goal. There was one boy, a bit taller than me with big cornrows in his hair. He was good, maybe better than good. I wanted to play with him, test him out, but we tried not to mix with gangs any more, even groups that just looked like gangs. We were wary.

As I watched the boy with the plaited hair score another goal, I had a great idea. Well, I thought it was a great idea.

'You know,' I said as I turned to Em, 'this ball could be worth a lot.' I held up the football.

Em had been lying down, but now he sat up and shielded his eyes from the weak winter sun. 'What?' he said.

'If it was signed by a famous footballer, kids would pay loads for it.'

'If it was, yeah,' my brother said, then lay back down.

'Well,' I continued, 'why don't I just sign it on

behalf of someone? Say, Juma Kwame.' Everyone loved the Arsenal captain, 'cos everyone round our way loved Arsenal, apart from a few glory-hunting Chelsea fans. 'I bet he'd love to help us, if he met us. We could get loads of balls and sign them by all of the Arsenal team. We'd make money in no time.'

Emmanuel coughed and raised an eyebrow at me. 'You know what Dad used to say?' I shrugged. Em continued. "If you don't have the money, you just have to walk away." We've gotta do this properly, Prince. It's important, I think.'

One of the boys at the far end of the pitch had lost control of their ball and it came skidding toward us.

'Over 'ere, mate,' one of them called.

I stood up and blasted the ball back, anger welling up in me, anger from a deep place. The same deep place that I heard my father's voice come from.

'I'll never let anything bad happen to you,' he'd said.

Bad things I could deal with, we'd had our share. But why could nothing good happen to us, not even a good idea?

Chapter 21

More than a week passed without a good plan coming to either of us. We didn't even have a bad plan.

We talked long into the night, passing whispers from bunk to bunk. Little crumbs of ideas that were quickly swept off the table for their impracticality, complexity or stupidity. Countless times I nearly suggested a return to crime, to picking pockets, to pinching stuff. The way I saw it, it was the easy way out. But I said nothing. I knew that my brother would refuse. Em was my moral compass. I didn't always follow him, but there he was all the same.

Some nights, as we lay awake thinking, or chatting about a new idea, we heard mum crying and sometimes talking. She wasn't on the phone though, and there was no one to comfort her.

We didn't speak about this. It scared me and I guess it scared Em too. We just carried on as usual. We went to school, ate with Mum, played with Grace, all the time trying to conjure a foolproof money-making scheme out of thin air. We were no magicians though.

It was a Tuesday when something finally stuck. A simple idea and, I thought, a brilliant one. English, next to art and music, was my worst subject. But that Tuesday, something made it more interesting.

Miss Strong had given us a bunch of cards with stuff on them. We had to decide if they were Science Fact or Science Fiction. I was sitting next to Albert, we were trying to decide together.

Albert is French so his name is not pronounced how you think it might be but I'm not sure how to write it otherwise. He was a bit weird. He loved English, especially reading. But then he only had his mum, like me, and she seemed, well, mad, so I could forgive him a bit of weirdness.

So, here you go, Science Fact or Science Fiction?

1.   You can make a clone of your pet. Science Fact. Miss Strong gave us ages to discuss it, even though we all knew that it was a fact. There was that sheep, Dolly or Dotty or something.

2.   There are devices that work like Harry Potter's invisibility cloak. Science Fiction. This one took us a bit longer, we didn't have any hard evidence, but it seemed impossible to us. We were right.

3.   Scientists have made something travel in time. We couldn't agree on this. Albert was certain that it couldn't be true. 'Otherwise, they'd have gone and got Shakespeare and made him write East-enders and television would be worth watching.' I laughed at this. Albert didn't. See, I told you he was weird.

Somewhere in my head a little bell was ringing. I was sure I had read something about time travel, something about tiny particles travelling milliseconds in time. I told Albert as much.

'No way,' he replied, still straight-faced. 'It's definitely Science Fiction.'

'I really think it's Science Fact.' That bell was ringing even louder.

'I bet you any money you like that it's Science Fiction.'

I ignored the bell and replayed what Albert had just said, 'any money you like'. I didn't have any money, but he didn't know that.

Miss Strong was counting down to when she would reveal if it was Fact or Fiction. 'Ten, nine, eight . . .'

'Fiver,' I quickly whispered to Albert.

'Seven . . .'

'What?'

' Six . . .'

'I'll bet you a fiver.'

'Five . . .'

'Erm.'

'Four, three . . . '

'Deal.' He stuck out his hand and we shook as the count-down ended. I crossed the fingers on my other hand.

'Science . . .' Miss Strong tapped the board, and "Fact" flashed up on the screen.

I cheered.

'You've been stealing again, haven't you?' was the first thing Em said when I showed him the loot.

'No,' I replied indignantly. 'I won this.'

We were in our room, having just arrived home from school. My brother was pulling off his school uniform, striped tie, white shirt. I sat on the bed.

'Won it?' he exclaimed, kicking his shoes off in my direction.

I told him about the bet. His glare made me stumble over my words. He didn't look pleased.

When I was finished, he took one more look at me before slipping on a T-shirt. 'Have I taught you nothing about staying out of trouble?' he said. 'You're doing this at school, Prince. What's wrong with you? What do you think it will do to Mum if you get caught?'

I didn't know what to say. Of course I had thought of the consequences. I had thought about losing lunch-times, getting lectured by teachers, at the worst, suspended from school. But I had not, for a moment, thought about Mum. What was wrong with me?

'Don't get caught,' Em said sternly. Then he laughed, snatching the note from my hand.

'Don't get caught!' I laughed right back.

That night, by the glare of the street lights that shone through our window, me and Em talked about how to spend the masses of money we'd certainly win.

'We're not buying you trainers,' my brother laughed.

I laughed along with him. The shoes didn't bother me so much now, they were just shoes, after all.

Em thought Grace should have some books.

'Definitely something for Grace,' I agreed. I wasn't sure about books though, maybe a ball.

'We should buy a nice take-away or something,' I suggested. 'Mum would love that.' Maybe I was trying to make up for my lack of sympathy for our mother earlier, or maybe the late-night talking reminded me of the tears we heard her shed.

On cue, the sound of muffled cries floated through the thin wall. This cut our conversation short. We said quick good nights, then tried to block out the sounds of sobbing.

This was not an easy task. The sobs were accompanied tonight by a word repeated over and over. I stopped trying to block out the noise and listened intently. One word. A word that reverberated around my mind. My dadda's name.

'Céléstin.'

I joined my mum in her weeping and fell asleep on a damp pillow.

Chapter 22

Ilala Market, Dar Es Salaam, Tanzania

The gangsters threatened, threw Céléstin's merchandise to the floor, slapped him around the face. Victor stood and watched. He must have recognised his brother but he showed no sign of it.

'Next time we're here we want some money,' the littlest man in the sharpest suit said. He usually did the talking.

Céléstin nodded. 'Yes, I will have some,' he said, knowing that there was no chance of this coming true. All the time he shot furtive glances at his younger brother.

'Victor,' the little man said, 'show him we mean business.'

Now Céléstin stared openly at Victor. Was that a tear that he saw escape below the rim of the glasses.

'I think he knows.' These were the first words Céléstin heard his brother say. They sent him into another coughing fit.

'What?' The little man glared at Victor, who towered above him. 'You're not here to think. I said, show him.'

Victor stepped forward, placed a hand on Céléstin's shoulders and planted his fist into his stomach all in one swift motion.

'Sorry,' Victor whispered, for his brother's ear only. And Céléstin knew as only a brother knows that the single sorry was meant for more than just the punch.

'Sorry I left,' Céléstin heard.

'Sorry I'm not looking after your boys.'

'Sorry we've ended up here.'

When Céléstin straightened, the gangsters were retreating into the market, taking Victor with them, just their backs on show.

'That was your brother?' Godwin said. He'd disappeared when the men had come close, but Céléstin did not blame him.

Instead he nodded, but that was all he could manage before a fresh bout of vicious coughs escaped his mouth. But something was different this time. He put his hands over his mouth and, when the fit was over, he looked down at fingers sprayed with blood.

Chapter 23

How much can you bet on around school?

Well, you'd be surprised.

That first day was slow going, just a dabble to test out the plan. I didn't have anything to lose, moneywise that is, so I couldn't bet anything big. However, from nothing at the start of the day, by the end I had eighteen big ones. And that was just from some small bets on a few races at lunch-time.

I had to keep it low-key. I knew the teachers wouldn't be happy. But then some of the teachers were never happy.

The next day, Wednesday, it took off. One pound became the standard stake. Before school I took seven bets on how many kids would be away that day. It was three. Only Eddie got it right so he doubled his pound. I kept the rest. Five more pounds taking me up to twenty-three.

In Maths I took bets on how many times Miss Strong would make a mistake on the board. Six, that's a lot, right? I thought teachers were meant to know everything. Eight kids bet on that and none of them got it right. I was up to thirty-one.

The playground was just as good. A race here, a game of four-square there, and I quietly added to my stash. I lost some but I won more. I had found something that looked like going right for once and by the end of Wednesday my winnings totalled forty-seven pounds and fifty pence. Not bad for two days' work, I thought.

I met Em outside the block of flats that was our new home.

I opened the front pocket of my school bag, the coins clinking as I shook it. My brother grinned.

'See,' I said, 'money equals happiness.'

Em laughed aloud and gave me a shove. Then he

threw his arm around me. Our grins got even wider as we headed up the long stairs.

We entered the flat, not to the sound of my mother's singing, but to weeping. Our grins fled.

That evening changed everything.

Through the weeping we could make out Grace's little cry. We threw our school bags down and my brother called out, 'Mum,' as we ran towards the kitchen. I had the worst thoughts of what was waiting behind that door. Blood, I saw a lot of blood in my mind. Fortunately I was wrong.

Our mum was sitting at the table, weeping and looking down at a few pieces of paper, scattered in front of her. Bills, they looked like, from the plain envelopes that nestled, ripped amongst them. The table cloth was scrunched up, gripped in her fists either side of the papers.

Grace, red-eyed, screaming, snot and tears mingling on her face, was sitting in her bouncy chair. A burning smell crept up our nostrils. Whatever had been on the hob was not going to make a good dinner.

I was gripped again by a feeling of confusion: that face, that laugh, even those tears, I knew so well, but so much about my mum was a mystery to me. I didn't move from the doorway.

Em was at my mother's side in a moment. He looked down at the letters, put his arm around our mum, then addressed me. 'Prince, take Grace.' I remained rooted to the spot until Em said my name again. 'Prince.'

I shook myself, then obeyed my brother, picking up my squirming sister.

She smelt. She smelt bad, bad enough to take my mind off the tears and the wailing, if only for a moment.

I pretended not to notice the smell as I went through to Grace and Mum's room; if I noticed, I'd have to change her nappy. No thanks.

She squirmed and cried, trying to wriggle free of my arms. It was like carrying a bag of snakes.

I laid her down on my mum's narrow bed. She screamed even more when she left my arms, a piercing wail that reverberated through my skull. If I wanted her to stop screaming, I had to change her. I knew that, but I still hesitated.

It's a messy business, changing a baby's nappy,

not something that I'd recommend. Someone's got to do it, though. I won't go into the squishy details, I don't want to gross you out.

Grace was much happier when she was clean and changed. She was the little brown lump that I was used to. With her big bright eyes, tiny squashed nose and tight curls of black hair, she was beautiful. Even I could admit that.

Unlike Emmanuel, I hadn't spent much time playing with my sister. But now I tickled her toes, made the kind of noises that my mum made for her and pretended to disappear over the side of the bed. She smiled every time I came back up. She smiled at me.

I looked around the room for some toys to amuse my new playmate. Pieces of clothing were scattered across the floor, a box of nappies stood in the corner by the rack where the clothes should have been hanging. Besides the bed that the baby lay on, and the half-empty rack, the only other bit of furniture was Grace's basket.

A ragged bear with one eye missing; a box of plastic squeaking eggs; a sock puppet Em had made, which was meant to be a duck. That was all my search turned up.

Something wasn't right here.

I tried to push the thought out of my mind as I pushed my hand into the sock puppet.

'Quack, Quack!' I continued to entertain Grace.

She gurgled and smiled at the misshapen duck as her hands and chubby arms flailed around in front of her. I smiled as well. The duck quacked at her hands, she pulled them away and clucked a short laugh. I laughed too. Her wide eyes searched around for something to focus on. She found my face. I stared right back.

My beautiful little sister was happy with an old sock to play with. Or was she happy with me? Money equals happiness? My theory was crumbling around me.

Chapter 24

Me and Grace played until Em interrupted us.

'Well done, Prince,' he said, looking over my shoulder at the smiling baby.

We both stared at the little bundle for a moment as I held her hand in mine.

'Is Mum OK?' I asked without turning round.

Em didn't answer, but let out a sigh. 'You got the money?' he asked.

I nodded, still looking at Grace. We could hear through the thin window pane a gang of boys and girls, blaring mobile phones, shouts and laughter. Probably the same gang that gathered near the entrance to our flats most days. Em and I stayed away.

'Would you go out and get some food, Prince?'

I turned around to look at my brother; concern was etched in his face.

'No worries, Em,' I replied.

I got chips and sausages from Oh My Cod. I laughed the first time I read that sign, while Em rolled his eyes and said, 'That's not funny.' It still makes me smile though.

When I got back, the gang outside our flat had swelled. Now they sprawled across the pavement, sitting and leaning against everything available. Some of them were smoking, others clutched drinks in their hands.

I took a deep breath; I didn't want trouble. But I needn't have worried. As I approached, I could see that they were all listening intently to a short, white guy. He stood out for three reasons: he was the only one not wearing a hood or cap, he had bright ginger hair, and he wasn't a teenager.

I stopped looking as I got closer. If you're smart, you don't look at anybody for too long around our way. Unless they're talking to you – then you'd better listen up. I stopped looking, but I tried my best to hear what the ginger man was talking to the gang about.

'What do you think life's all about?' he was saying. 'Having as much fun as you can?' I kept walking, but craned to hear more of the speech. 'Making as much money? Do any of those things make you happy?'

I don't know, I thought, as I entered the building and fell out of earshot. I had been sure they did, but now. . .

Before I put my key in the lock I could hear singing. My mum was singing again. She greeted me at the door with a kiss on the head and a hug. I smiled.

'Thank you, my little Prince,' she sang, her voice rising at the end of my name.

'OK, Mum.' I pulled away from the hug and hung my coat up.

A sing-song voice, a kiss, a hug and happiness had crept back in. Happiness tinged by worry, fear, confusion, but it was there all the same.

We ate our chips and sausages quietly, apart from the occasional verse of song from our mum. Em ate one-handed, Grace perched on his knee. She gurgled and grabbed at the colourful plastic tablecloth like a moth attracted to a flame.

Em and I went to our room after dinner.

'So, what's going on?' I asked, kicking at the football that sat on our floor. If anything I was more confused than ever. Can you go from being sad to sing-song happy, just like that?

Em slumped down on his bunk as I started to do kick-ups. It's much more difficult in a cramped bedroom and I enjoyed the challenge, you couldn't let the ball touch any of the walls or furniture. You should try it sometime – don't tell your parents I said that, though.

Em was silent for a while, watching me keep the ball in the air.

'Come on, spit it...' I nearly lost control of the ball, but some quick footwork and a long stretch kept it from colliding with the bunk-beds, 'out.'

'It's Father,' my brother finally said. 'He's in trouble . . .'

I let the ball drop to the floor.

'He's in Africa still, Tanzania, and he's in trouble. He owes some men a lot of money.'

As the ball bounced under the bed, I suddenly knew what our happiness depended on.

'We've got to get him, Em.'

My brother stared at me for a moment then nodded.
'We've got to get him.'

Chapter 25

It cost my parents all they had to send us away. Everything. They sold their home. They gave up their safety. They broke their hearts.

I was angry with my parents for sending us away. I was desperately sad. But now I know what it cost.

The morning we left, they left too. Their part of Katanga was no longer safe. Bullets reigned. Terrible things happened, things I won't write about, things I don't want to think about. But they happened all the same.

They went to my grandmother's house first, in a village, and lived a life much like the one they'd fled. Here they lingered for around a year before the violence caught up with them. Nana would not leave. She had lived in that one room all her life but she insisted her son and his wife make themselves safe.

So my parents headed east, towards the rising sun and Lake Tanganyika. For months they walked, eating only what they could find, and all the while my mother's stomach swelled and their journey became slower.

Finally they stopped, on the edge of the great lake of blue and green and brown. Here my father worked. One month's work on a fishing boat bought them passage across the lake to Tanzania. For that month they ate well, feasting on fish, and the baby grew larger still. By the time the month was up my mother was a hippo (this is Remy's own description).

Everyone knows giving birth is terrible. Giving birth on a boat, doubly so. Giving birth on a boat in a storm, well, you'd need to ask my mother about that.

Grace, they named her. For only by God's grace had she made it into the world, that's what my father said.

Maybe he was right. After the tumultuous passage across the lake their fortune turned. The boat's captain, my father's employer, took pity on Céléstin, Remy and my new little sister. He contacted his brother who lived nearby. This brother's business was haulage. He took the fish from the lake all over Tanzania, occasionally even as far as Dar Es Salaam.

So, stinking of fish, half-frozen by the packed ice, jolted and jarred by the bumpy road, my parents arrived in Tanzania's capital. Far away, their sons were arriving in another capital. Now, the parents and the sons found themselves with no money, nowhere to call home and no one to call on for help. Aid, however, did eventually come. A certain Mr Green took me and Em under his wing, whilst in Africa my parents found gangsters of their own to help them.

My father took on the debt which now held him captive. In exchange the gangsters arranged passage to London for my mother. Here, she would begin her search for us.

My father knew that the debt was insurmountable, that he would be paying the "businessmen" for a very long time. But once again he paid all he had to see us safe, everything. He sold himself. He gave up his wife and daughter.

Now it was our turn to see him safe. And what could we give but everything we had.

Chapter 26

How could we get my father back?

I ate my porridge slowly, thinking. Mum was singing again at breakfast, feeding Grace and twiddling Em's hair.

I walked to school slowly, thinking. George didn't knock for me, I didn't live on his route any more. He would have been proud of me though, I saw things in the clouds that day: my mother's smile, Grace's sock puppet duck and a large, dark hand I knew to be my father's.

I did my lessons slowly, thinking. Miss Strong made me talk to her at break-time.

'Is everything OK, Prince?' she asked. 'Everything

121

OK at home?'

For years me and Em had practised not talking to teachers or doctors or policemen; it was a hard habit to stop. I forced my practised smile and told her that I was fine. 'Just a bit tired,' I said.

Lunchtime gave me a break from thinking. I ate with George and played pat-ball; I was still banned from the football pitch, my main punishment after the fight.

We did art in the afternoon; I went back to thinking. We were doing still-life. Miss Strong had put a bowl of fruit on all the tables and we'd made these square things called view-finders. Most people's drawings were round and shaded skilfully to look like the spheres they were meant to be. Mine was all jagged angles and scrawled shading. I had started again twice, but this was still my best attempt.

I didn't care though, I had something more important on my mind – how to get my father back.

After all my thinking I came to the conclusion that maybe my first theory wasn't so wrong. Money, that's what we needed. If we had money, we could get him back. If we had money, we'd be happy. Money equals happiness.

+ + +

There wasn't much to them, the shops near our flats. Two of them were boarded up, one that used to be a barber's called Toni's, and the other without a sign, newspaper plastered to the inside of the windows. Along with these and Oh My Cod, our chippy, there was a shop that sold flowers, although they can't have sold many, half the ones in the window were usually dead. Then there was Rahman's Food and Wine, a shop that sold everything from newspapers to tins of beans, and a little post office.

In the wall by the post office was a cash machine. An old lady with white hair, sandals with socks, and a handbag with a strap that was too long for her body, was waiting behind a tall man. We saw them as we approached.

Em had pointed out the old lady from the end of the road and said, 'What about her?' playing our usual game.

'Um, she's called . . .' it took me a while to think what kind of names old ladies had. 'Dot?' I said.

'Ha.' Em laughed at this, as we walked toward the white-haired lady. 'That's from that programme.'

As Em spoke, the man finished at the cash machine

and walked into the post office. "Dot" stepped forward, fumbling around in her bag.

'Maybe,' I replied to my brother, knowing that I definitely had stolen the name from a television programme. 'She's retired,' I continued, 'and lives in a flat with six cats and two dogs.'

Em laughed again. We were about ten steps away from "Dot" now. Her fumbling had located a black purse which, even from a distance, we could see was worn and battered.

Nine steps away and the old lady opened the purse. Eight steps and she took out her card. Seven, she reached behind her, attempting to place the purse back in the still open bag. Six, the purse dropped to the floor. At five steps I felt something that I only felt in two situations, when I stood in front of goal, ready to shoot, or when I was going to steal something, the two things I'd been best at in life.

It started with a tightening of the chest, and my breathing became short and sharp. My mind focused, all distractions gone, and I could see only the spot I would place the ball, or the object of my theft. The world slowed down, not like slow-motion in a film, I guess it was more like I sped up.

Before Em could speak or "Dot" could turn round,

before I even had time to think, I was a hunter. The last five steps I covered quickly. Stooping as I ran, my fingers traced the pavement till they made contact with the scratched leather. Then they closed around my prey.

I straightened up, my legs ready for an all-out sprint, then . . .

Thump, crack, everything went dark.

Em had been shouting at me to stop – he didn't want to go back to stealing. As I stooped, the tall man from the cash machine came out of the post office. He watched me as I watched the purse. He saw me as I picked it off the floor. He knew what I'd do next so he stuck out his arm.

I crashed into it. My own speed sent me spinning to the floor and my head made a vicious noise against the pavement.

It turned out he wasn't just a tall man, he was a tall policeman.

Chapter 27

Grey walls, a most uninviting grey. A grey, metal door, with a small grille set into it for communicating and passing food through. A metal framed bed attached to the wall, a thin, hard mattress on top covered by a coarse grey blanket, no pillow. This was my cell.

I picked at the blanket, pulling off loose bobbles of fibre, balling them together. I studied the wall, following the lines of painted brickwork, staring intensely at any crack or frozen line of dripped paint. I paced the floor, kicking at each wall as I reached the end of my very short route.

I imagined Em explaining to Mum what had happened. She cried. She wasn't angry, in my mind, but terribly sad.

'Why would he do this?' she would ask and Em would explain the plan to get Dad back. Mum would cry even more. She'd forbid it too, I was sure of that.

'My boys.'

She'd lost us once before.

I thought about Bigger, from Africa, who'd lost everything. I thought about trying to be happy. I thought about a blurred face, like an older version of my brother rearing up at me. I felt strong arms go around me. I heard my father's laughter.

'Clunk, clunk.' Something metal rapped at the door and brought me quickly out of my daydream. The grate slid open with a squeak. A rectangular portion of face could be seen, eyes, nose and the top lip – features that belonged to the police officer who had shown me to the cell.

'Come on then,' he called through the slit. 'Get your stuff.'

I looked around. I had no 'stuff'. I stood up, shrugging my jacket back on. The keys rasped in the lock as I clomped across the floor. Then the metal door swung open.

'You're lucky, son,' the police officer said. 'You'd be staying at least a night, if we didn't need this cell.'

I just stared at him. Lucky, was I? I couldn't remember a time when I'd really been lucky.

He led me down the corridor. As we passed several more cell doors he explained that I'd have to appear in court, that I would receive a summons, a letter asking you to come to court, but that I'd probably get away with community service.

There were lots of forms to fill out before I could leave. I waited in an office, as the policeman scribbled furiously. Being a policeman, it seemed, was not like it looked on TV.

I had assumed Em would be waiting for me. This is what I thought about as I watched the form being filled in: his scowl, his disappointed look as he walked away, leaving me to follow. I didn't think my mum would be there, despite the scene I'd played out in my head earlier. Neither of them, though, were in the lobby when I finally emerged. But there was somebody waiting.

I had my head down as the officer led me out, through a heavy door. I heard someone rise from one of seats round the edge of the lobby, but all I saw was a pair of familiar, shiny, man-sized shoes.

'What have you been up to, Prince?' Jubrel asked.

Chapter 28

I had missed Ruth and Jubrel, after we moved in with our mother. I'd spoken to Ruth on the phone a few times, and Em had been to see Alice. They had new foster kids which felt a bit weird.

I admit it – I was jealous. Now, don't go shouting about this. I'm a boy after all, but I think I had begun to love Ruth and Jubrel. They were always smiling, always ready to talk to me, always there with a gentle word. And, most importantly, when I lived with them, I didn't have to worry about money or food or terrible shoes.

'I think you've got taller, Prince,' Jubrel said in his deep voice. We sat opposite each other, chips and drinks between us. Jubrel had taken me to fast food restaurants before when we'd needed to talk.

I smiled at him, taking in his greying hair and smooth face. He was as warm as ever. I told him all that had happened, not why, just what, on the way to the restaurant and he made me forget it almost straight away. He was magic like that, Jubrel.

Now Jubrel was ready with some questions.

How was I getting on?

Fine, school was as boring as ever.

Was I getting on any better with my teacher?

I'd had some problems with Miss Strong at the start. She thought I was a trouble-maker and I thought she was something that I won't repeat here. Things were OK now though.

How was Em?

Good, but still rubbish at football.

Then I had some questions of my own.

How did Jubrel know where I was?

Em had called him.

How was Ruth?

Mad as ever.

Me and Jubrel both laughed at this.

What were the new foster kids like?

A boy and a girl, a bit rough but lovely. The boy reminded him of me when I first arrived. They'd be going soon though.

I was pleased that they weren't staying long; I was definitely jealous.

Then Jubrel asked the killer question we'd both avoided.

'Is it going OK with Mum and all the changes?'

'Fine,' I said.

'Fine?' Jubrel replied. 'Fine doesn't get you into a police cell, Prince.'

I'd finished my chips a long time ago but picked up the packet for something to do, anything rather than meet Jubrel's eye.

He snatched the packet off me and I nearly reacted, my temper rising, but now he had me. I was looking right at him.

'OK,' I said, a tear beginning to form. 'It's rubbish.'

I told him about having no money, the trainers, Grace's lack of toys.

'A lot of people struggle to make ends meet, Prince,' was his response.

I told him about the tears, Mum's and mine.

He nodded and asked if I knew what was making Mum so sad.

So, finally, I told him about my father, about the debt. But I did not mention our plan.

He put down his paper coffee cup before replying, 'Prince, I'm sorry.' I nodded as he spoke, looking up at his warm face. 'I'm so sorry. I wish there was something we could do, anything. But I don't think I know a way to help you.'

I nearly told him the plan then, nearly asked him for money, even to come with us. But I knew that he wouldn't approve. He'd talk about letting go, moving on, trying to be happy with what we've got. So I said nothing and Jubrel drove me home.

When we parted, outside the flats, he said it again. 'If there's anything, Prince, anything we can do, please just come knocking.'

Then it hit me. There was something Jubrel could do.

Chapter 29

I hadn't thought it through. Not carefully enough anyway. I thought, with the key, we'd be in and out in no time. Stupid, that's what I was, I'd forgotten all about the chain. I don't know how I'd forgotten it. Ruth always said that she couldn't sleep without the chain on. More than once, I'd listened to her pleading with Jubrel to go down and check it.

'Go on you cruel, cruel man, you'd leave your poor woman's house defenceless.'

Jubrel would go in the end, the stairs creaking beneath him.

So Em and his stupid brother stood in front of the house, the door ajar. All that remained between us and tickets to our father was a metal chain.

It had taken me a long time to persuade Em to come. But eventually I had convinced him it was just a loan. We'd repay it as soon as we could.

'What do we do now?' Em hissed.

It was dark, the street lights making circles up and down the pavement. We were in shadow. Two o'clock in the morning was an eerie time to be out. All we'd seen on the way over was a mangy fox. It stalked across the road, paying us no more notice than it did the parked cars.

To each side of the door were small windows, stained glass on the right and frosted on the left. Ruth had told me that they both used to be stained glass. They'd had to break one when they'd locked themselves out. So I knew what to do.

I placed my hand on the glass and mimed for Em's benefit.

He considered the glass for a moment, scratched his head, then nodded. 'Do it,' he whispered.

So I did.

The night's chill silence was shattered as the glass fell away. I nearly added a cry to the crash; I'd struck the window with my palm and didn't need to hold it up to the distant street light's glow to know that it was cut, badly. My thumb throbbed, each pulse a wave of pain. I bit down hard.

We listened for a moment. No sound. It seemed our breaking had gone unnoticed. Now for the entering. I thrust my bleeding hand through the jagged, toothed opening, taking care not to slice it further. It was not a long reach round to the catch. I unhooked it and we were in.

I feared the stairs. Their ominous creaking could be our undoing. We took each one slowly, trying to put as much weight as we could on to the banister, pushing ourselves up more than stepping. Slowly, slowly we made our way to the top.

On the landing, we stopped and listened. Em's breathing was heavy behind me. In the distance a siren sounded. We couldn't hear a peep from further into the house. Normally Jubrel's snores could be heard throughout the building. I was surprised that all was quiet.

A minute passed before I beckoned my brother forward. Thankfully the door to the study swung open soundlessly. Here, Em waited. He was the ears now.

I crept on. A photo of my former carers glared down at me from the wall and my own beaming face was framed on the desk along with a host of other children.

The filing cabinet was opposite the large photo of Ruth and Jubrel. I was thankful that I could turn my back on their accusatory look, but as soon as I did my shoulders prickled. I felt as if I was being watched.

At first I fumbled with the dials, squinting in the dark to pick out the miniscule numerals. It felt like minutes before I had the first number.

1

The second one came easier, even though my hands were damp with sweat.

1

As I tried to find the next, my brother entered the room and pulled the door to behind him.

'Prince,' he whispered into the gloom. 'That siren, I'm pretty sure it's coming this way.'

I didn't answer. What was there to say? Besides, I nearly had the third number.

2

I could hear the siren myself now, and a car, screeching down the road. My hands began to shake. Car doors slammed and the final dial clicked into place.

0

I yanked open the top drawer, quickly grasped the passports and slammed it shut.

'Police!' a voice yelled from downstairs as I slid the passports into my pocket and Em swore. 'Show yourselves.'

I pulled at the second drawer. It jammed, the top drawer still slightly open. I pushed, pulled, reached in and grasped the wooden box.

A light went on downstairs as my brother whispered, 'What do we do now?'

Have you ever had one of those crisis moments where everything just happens? You don't need to think, your brain and your body act as one. This was definitely one of those.

Without a word to my brother I reached for the window clasp, unlocked it and wrenched the pane open. The stairs began to creak.

I jumped.

The five minutes before had rocketed by, but now as I hung in the air, I had a moment of clarity. Of course we'd woken Ruth and Jubrel with the breaking glass and, being sensible, they'd phoned the police.

For a second time I was thankful. If my foster carer had taken it on himself to chase us off, he would definitely have recognised me. That was the last thing I wanted.

I careered into the bushes below. I had aimed carefully and the shrubbery broke my fall. I was quickly on my feet, the wooden box clutched to my chest. My brother crash-landed behind me, swearing again, this time loudly. He, too, got up, but hobbled as we raced down the garden.

Em, injured, needed a bunk over the fence and cried out as he landed on the other side. I hauled myself over to another shout of 'Police,' this time followed by 'Stop!'

We didn't.

Ruth and Jubrel's garden backed on to another. We ran towards the house that loomed above us in the dark, and down the side alley. For a third time that night I gave thanks. The gate at the end was bolted, but not locked.

We couldn't run fast – Em's ankle was hurting him badly. But we ran fast enough. Before we knew it we were gasping for breath at the bottom of our flats with no sounds of pursuit to be heard.

We'd done it. We were thieves again.

Chapter 30

There is an infectious disease that is so common that one in three people on our planet carry it. That means if there are 30 children in your class, 10 of them have it. The good news is that only one in 10 of those infections will go on to become the active disease. The bad news is that the one classmate who does have the disease has only a 50/50 chance of surviving on his own. Around 2,000,000 people die from this disease every year. That's about 10 for every letter in this book. It's a killer.

Once upon a time it was called consumption. People thought it consumed the sufferer from the inside out. One of its main symptoms is weight loss and paleness. Sufferers may also have a fever and often feel tired. But by far the most common symptom is a persistent cough accompanied by blood.

Tuberculosis, the disease is called, also known as TB, and it can be treated. That's why no one you know has got it. But people in the Developing World, in places like Africa, die from it all the time. They just can't afford the drugs they need to survive.

Chapter 31

Ilala Market, Dar Es Salaam, Tanzania

Worry flitted at the edge of Céléstin Anatole's mind. He had a lot to worry about. His wife was alone in a strange country with his baby daughter. The man who had promised to protect his sons was not doing his job. He was in debt to pitiless gangsters. And now this, the blood.

Every day since he'd seen his brother, Victor, the man whose broken promise added to his worries, the man who counted himself amongst his debt collectors, he'd coughed up more blood.

But Céléstin had a misson. Worry would not stop him. He was consumed with one question. It burned in his mind.

'Where are my sons?'

He put this question to his friend, Godwin, for what seemed like the hundredth time.

'There is only one man who can tell you,' Godwin replied. 'You know that, Céléstin. You must wait. Patience.'

Céléstin was angry, as he had been almost constantly since his meeting with Victor. 'Don't tell me to wait. Don't tell me to be patient. Don't tell me all will be well, GOD WILLING!'

Several other stall-holders turned for a moment to shake their heads or tut in Céléstin's direction. He ignored them. Godwin did not. He bowed and bobbed and begged apologies on all sides.

'My friend, I am sorry,' he said, turning back, 'but what more can I say? You must wait for the men to come with your brother. You must ask him the question.'

This conversation was repeated at Céléstin's stall many times over the days that passed. Godwin thought about not turning up for their ritualistic chat, but he could not bring himself to deprive a man in need.

All the same, Céléstin was surprised when the Tanzanian stall-holder came running to him one day, towards the end of trading. 'They are here, my brother,' he called, a grin stretched across his face.

Céléstin looked past his running friend, towards the market entrance, and there, as Godwin had promised, was the black car he'd come to recognise.

In his mind, he had practised what happened next. He left his stall, without a word to Godwin, the table crashing as he ran back into the market. A little way in, he turned left. A little further on, maybe fifty metres, he turned left again, heading back towards the entrance.

At this moment, if his plan was to work, the gangsters, including Victor, would be in the market, searching for him. If his plan was to work, none of the gangsters would be waiting by their car. If his plan was to work, a taxi would be loitering, ready to take shoppers home.

The plan worked. He leapt into a battered yellow taxi, coughing into a handkerchief.

'Where to, my friend?' the driver asked, turning to face Céléstin. His smile showed only five teeth still in his head and his hair was all straggles of white and grey.

'I want you to follow that car.' Céléstin had thought he would feel silly delivering that line and he was right! As he pointed at the gangsters' vehicle, a grin crept across his face in spite of the situation.

'That car?' the driver asked, pointing to the sleek black vehicle.

'Yes, yes,' Céléstin replied.

'That one that's just sitting there?'

'Yes.'

The driver considered this a moment, looking from his passenger to the car in question. 'I will have to charge you for the sitting,' he said.

'Whatever it costs,' Céléstin replied, hoping that it would not cost more than the little he'd saved, a wedge of notes in various currencies, nestled in his shoe.

The wait seemed short, the journey longer. Céléstin was sure that Victor and his friends would spot the car that tailed them. His heart froze when the vehicle stopped and the taxi driver pulled in directly behind it.

'What are you doing?' the white-haired driver asked as he turned to collect his fare and saw his passenger squashed into the foot-well, coughing.

'They must not see me,' Céléstin hissed.

'Oh,' the driver said, nodding. 'Well, I'll have to charge you for this too.'

They had stopped to let out one of the gangsters, the little one with the sharpest suit. Victor did not emerge and the car quickly took off again. Céléstin's taxi followed.

When the gangsters stopped again, the driver knew the deal. He parked a safe distance away, and Céléstin watched as the familiar figure of his brother clambered out of the car.

'I'll get out here,' he told the driver. 'How much do I owe you?'

'How much have you got, my friend?' the driver croaked.

Céléstin pulled out every one of his notes but before he could begin to count the driver said, 'That will do.'

He looked down at the money, then handed over all he had. Céléstin mourned its loss with a single sigh. Another worry joined the others at the edge of his mind.

But his mission was nearly complete. His worries could wait.

Chapter 32

It had seemed like a great idea. Easy money. I had a key, I knew where the loot was. Quick and easy. But, like the chain, there was something else I hadn't thought about. How do you sell an antique gun? Cos we didn't need a gun, we needed money.

It had been a Friday night when the robbery took place, so we had a whole weekend to think. We spent the morning jumping at every sound, convinced that Jubrel or the police would be knocking on the door any minute. But when no one arrived, we did what we always do. We played football. It was as we argued that another problem hit me.

'When we sell the gun…'

'If we sell it,' Em corrected as we left the park.

'Whatever, when, if, you know what I mean!' The late night and the arguing had taken their toll and my temper was bubbling just below the surface.

'Once we have the money,' I tried again, 'how do we get the tickets?'

'What do you mean?' Em asked.

I dodged a large pile of dog's mess before I answered. 'Well, who sells plane tickets to children?'

Em frowned and bounced the football hard. 'So,' he said as we reached the flats, 'we need to find someone who will buy the . . .' my brother looked around a moment, 'you know what, and someone who will buy us plane tickets.'

We both sighed.

We were in too deep. We walked on, homewards. Em sighed again.

'We need a criminal,' I muttered, thinking of Mr Green, the malevolent gang leader who used to tell us what to steal, and sell what we got our hands on.

'A criminal,' Em muttered right back.

We walked on a few more steps.

'A criminal!' I repeated. 'What about Frankie?'

'Frankie?' Em said, raising an eyebrow. He knew exactly who I meant.

George's estate was a dangerous place. You

didn't show your face around there unless you were known. Even my friend had taken a few beatings before he was recognised. The most important person to be recognised by, the man who ruled the estate, was a tattooed gangster called Frankie. Most people around our way knew who he was.

'We want to make money, Prince, not lose blood,' Em said.

I didn't reply.

The day rolled by and no fresh ideas came to us. For the kind of help we needed, there was no one to turn to. Mum kept asking if we were OK.

'Yeah, yeah, we're fine, Mum,' we replied.

The evening came, and we were itching for action.

I pushed open the door to our bedroom. Em was playing with Grace, using the sock-puppet and putting on silly voices. Outside the sun was setting, and a wash of orange light filled the room. I slumped on to my brother's bed.

'OK,' Em said, 'we'll go to Frankie.'

My brother and sister both looked up at me. 'You sure?' I replied.

Em shook his head. 'No,' he said, 'but have you got a better idea?'

The block of flats George lived in was just like ours. It was just like all the flats in our area. Not really tall like the ones you see in films, tall enough, but mostly wide, sprawling across an area big enough to get lost in if you didn't know your way around. I knew it well enough. I knew how to get to George's and stay out of trouble. I knew how to get into trouble too.

I thought about my warm bed and my safe room, with Mum asleep in the next room. Then I pulled my jacket close around me before leading Em into the maze of brick and concrete.

We heard trouble before we saw it, the tinny sound of music blaring out of mobile phones, the latest Lil' Legacy track, voices, laughter. I thought there must be four, maybe five, men gathered just around the next corner. We stopped. Could we go through with this? My heart was pounding.

Em stepped forward first. I followed.

There were more guys than I had expected, I think I counted ten, gathered around the brick stairwell that led deeper into the flats. Dark jackets covered white T-shirts that shone as brightly as their white trainers. Most had caps too, black with gold, or white with gold. Two sat on mopeds even though we were far off the road, the others leaned against walls or slouched on steps. Their cigarettes glowed orange in the darkness.

We had approached silently and it was a few moments before anyone noticed us.

'Who the . . . are you?' one of the men on the steps said, a heavy gold chain hung around his neck.

My mouth was dry and clamped shut. A large dog, sitting on the floor beside one of the men, began to growl, then sat up on its haunches. I hadn't seen the dog before. Now I saw another, stepping out of the shadows of a moped.

Have I mentioned that me and Em hate dogs? It was a fear that came from some awful memory I didn't want to recall.

I thought about running, but Em, much braver than me, opened his mouth. 'We're no one,' he said. 'We just . . .' my brother eyed the dogs that had begun to strain at their leashes, both growling, a mass of slathering, bloodthirsty teeth, 'we just want to . . . to see Frankie.'

A couple of the men laughed, the dogs started to bark, and the gold-chained man who had spoken first flicked his cigarette butt in our direction, the burning ember flying through the air.

'Why would he want to see you?' he said.

Again my feet itched to be away and again my brother opened his mouth, 'We've got something he'll . . . he will want.' He only stuttered once this time.

'Show me,' the man said.

Em looked at me but my eyes were too busy to return his glance, flicking from one dog to the other, my knees shaking.

'Show him,' I muttered.

The men shifted, perhaps to get a glimpse of what we'd brought, perhaps ready to pounce. One of the dogs wrenched at its leash and I nearly stumbled backwards. My brother reached into his jacket pocket, several other hands went to pockets. I raised a foot, ready to sprint.

Gasps were the first response to the ancient gun, followed by a new round of laughter from several of the men. Then they relaxed back to their positions and the moped dog slunk into the shadows.

'What is that old piece of crap?' one of the men exclaimed.

The gold-chained man still sat, considering us.

'What you expecting Frankie to give you for that?'

he said, motioning at the antique in Em's hands.

My mouth was still glued shut so my brother replied. 'Erm,' he began. 'Plane tickets.' New snorts of laughter reverberated around the men. Em pressed on. 'Plane tickets to Dar Es Salaam, Tanzania. The next flight available.' He had mastered his stutter.

The gold-chained man looked at the gun, at his friends, then back to us. The second dog had sat down. Most of the men were ignoring us.

'I gotta say, boys, you got guts,' the gold-chained man said. 'I certainly think Frankie will be surprised. Give it here then, we'll see if it's worth something.'

Em looked at me again. I shrugged. We couldn't trust this man, but we certainly couldn't refuse him. My brother stepped forward and I could see his knees nearly give way. The gun, our only chance of making enough money, changed hands.

'Where can I find you?' the man said.

Em began to speak, but I quickly interrupted, I didn't want these men knowing where we lived.

'I go to Yerville School,' I blurted out.

'Now,' the man leant forward as he spoke, 'run away, before this dog eats you!' With that he kicked the lying dog in the ribs. Instantly it leapt forward, rage in its eyes and my feet finally had their way. We tore through the estate, followed by hungry barks.

Chapter 33

Doctoring a passport is hard.

First, the plastic that covers the main page is stuck down so tight that in order to take it off, you have to rip the page apart. You can try using a really sharp knife (we had my mum's best kitchen knife, not ideal), but even with that you won't get between the plastic and the paper.

If you do manage to peel off the plastic, the whole page is covered with a kind of hologram, printed over the top of the photo, writing, everything. There is no way to replicate this, no way we could think of anyway.

I'm sure that there are people out there who could

have done a good job forging us passports, but we had no money, and now, no gun. We were on our own.

Every day, after school, while we waited for news of the plane tickets, news that I was sure was not going to come, we got out Ruth and Jubrel's passports and thought about the problem. We couldn't just use them as they were, the photos were such a big give-away. Even the laziest of inspectors would see that Emmanuel was not a middle-aged lady.

We thought about dressing up. Em even tried on some of Mum's clothes, when she was out of course. But we both laughed so hard that we knew we wouldn't be able to keep a straight face.

In the end we made an OK job of it.

I took some sticky-back plastic out of Miss Strong's desk drawer and a better, sharper knife. Em borrowed a camera from school. 'There's loads,' he said, 'no one will miss it for a few days.' For the photos, we made a backdrop from our cleanest sheet, and put our most serious faces on. Em printed the results out at school too.

Carefully, we cut the sticky-back plastic to size, gradually trimming it to shape. We stuck the photo over the top of the existing one and applied the plastic.

The result was a long way from perfect. But we hoped that, from a glance, we wouldn't be detected.

If anyone read the passports, I was still forty-six and my brother was called Ruth. Like I said, they were a long, long way from perfect.

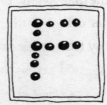

Chapter 34

Eastern Katanga, Democratic Republic of Congo, four years ago

Creating things has never been my strong point. Making stuff is hard. Even back home I knew I was no good. I only have one memory of making something I was proud of.

It happened at a rare event. The whole family were together: me and Em, my mother and father, uncle Victor and my grandmother. My dad and Victor had driven her over from her village. I think it was a special birthday, maybe hers.

Before they arrived, Mum had set me and Em a challenge. 'Can you make Grandma a special picture using stones?' she'd said, then shown us by placing lines of stones to make a square.

Em had probably grinned broadly at this. He was the creative one, not me. He could turn his hand to most things. That's how it went. Em was the maker, I was the athlete.

He turned his hand to this too. I can still remember the portrait that he painted across the cracked ground in front of our house, a portrait of Nana herself. Mum smiled and kissed his head.

For my efforts I had a scattering of stones and a fuming rage. I did not understand why I was so useless with my hands. It didn't matter to me, in that moment, that I was so useful with my feet. Em tried to help but I only shouted at him. My mother tried too and I calmed a little.

When they arrived, Nana, Dad and Victor all cooed over Em's picture. I stood back, wishing I could do something that I never would be able to. Mother whispered in my father's ear, then led my elderly grandma, Victor and Em away.

My dad hung back. 'Yours did not go so well, I hear,' he said, putting his arm around my shoulders.

I didn't answer but looked down at my feet, dark, even against the brown earth.

'What about a sum, Prince?' my father said, 'You are so good at maths.'

I looked up at him, puzzled, until he explained.

I spent an age placing the rocks in careful lines, each as accurate as the last, writing my chosen sum on to the ground.

When we called the family back out, they cooed just as loudly over my work as for Em's.

I beamed as I read it aloud.

'Fun plus love equals family.'

Chapter 35

That was a strange few days, carrying on as normal, going to school, chatting with Mum, playing with Grace. But all the while waiting, waiting for some sort of reply. Most of the time, I was certain we'd never hear from Frankie or the guy with the gold chain. I was sure that the gun was gone. I think Em shared my gloom, but he didn't let on.

Occasionally, a sense of hope broke through the doubt only to be squashed by the worry that Jubrel, Ruth or the police might show up at any minute. I had a sneaking suspicion that they knew it was us, knew we'd taken the gun. Maybe they'd decided this was the way to help us, not dobbing us in.

It was a Friday when the waiting ended. Fridays in school were a mixed bag. We had PE, but Mr Alan who took our lesson was always in a bad mood. He was safe most of the time, but not Friday afternoon.

We did basketball. It wasn't football, but still, I wasn't too bad. We had a free-throw competition at the end. By the last throw, my team had four points and George's had four too. Everyone else was out of it, with only one or two. Me and my friend had the final shots.

We played on the pitch that was right next to the road. It was nearly the end of the day and a few parents were waiting to pick up their kids. I like a crowd, so does George.

He went first, his team clapping and cheering, a few of mine heckling. My friend didn't mind. He casually flicked the ball into the net.

'Yes!' His team screamed.

'Your turn, buddy,' George grinned, placing the ball in my hands.

I stepped up to the line, balanced the ball on my right hand above my head, supported with my left then turned to give my team a wink. I took a breath when something glinted in the corner of my eye, a flash of gold on black.

I fumbled my shot, the ball smacking into the back-board and striking the hoop before bouncing away.

'That was a brick, Prince,' Mr Alan said. 'You're better than that.'

I smiled at the teacher, who smiled back, before looking for the glimmer that had been so offputting. I hoped to see Frankie and his gold-chained friend peering through the bars beside the pitch, but there was just the same gaggle of mums. No sign of gold.

All the same, I was sure I'd seen something and my hopes were high. I didn't even mind when George's team celebrated right under my nose.

'Too bad,' my friend said, clapping me on the shoulder.

When home-time came, I darted through the thronging mass of parents and children that filled the playground, through the open school gates and on to the street. I looked down the road both ways, to see even more parents heading towards school. My heart sank again.

If someone's sad in class, Miss Strong always says, 'Someone send for a taxi, so-and-so's in the doldrums.' That's where I was, The Doldrums.

I trudged towards home, not even bothering to wait and see if Em was meeting me. He probably wouldn't. We'd not been talking much over the previous few days because we'd only depressed each other more.

I was nearly at the end of the road when I noticed a car following me, a small blue car with shiny wheels and a black windscreen. I tried not to stare, it looked like the kind of car that played loud music, the kind of car you stayed away from.

Little by little, as I quickened my pace, the car pulled up alongside me and, sure enough, I could hear the thump, thump of music inside.

'Slow down, boy,' a voice called, a voice that I recognised.

I turned to see the gold-chained gangster hanging out the passenger side of the small car. I couldn't help myself. I smiled.

'School must have got better since I went,' the man said. 'I don't remember smiling.'

My grin slid away as he continued. 'You know how much that thing was worth, boy?'

I shook my head in reply.

'You've made us a tidy packet.'

He paused here but I had nothing to say. We'd both come to a standstill and I looked up and down the street again. What would people think of this conversation?

'Frankie says you can have what you asked for.' The man held out a kind of envelope, white and blue card. 'Looks like you're going to wherever that place is. You leave on Sunday.'

My grin returned, twice as big, and I didn't think anything would wipe it off now. I managed to croak a 'thank-you'.

'What's that, Frank?' the passenger said, leaning in to talk to the driver. 'Frankie says he's put a little something in for you too.' This time he spoke to me.

'Are you OK there, Prince?' A voice called behind me.

I turned to see Mr Alan approaching, as the screech of tyres announced the criminals' departure.

My teacher's eyes, from ten paces away, looked straight at the envelope I held in my hand, then up at me with a suspicious look in his eyes. I looked straight back down at the tickets. I was taking no chances. I turned and ran.

I flew home, my grin growing with every step. We'd done it. We were leaving on Sunday.

Chapter 36

The night before, we didn't sleep much. We'd dressed ready to leave, packed, squashing things into bags, talked and worried. We did two really important things too.

'How are we gonna find him?' I asked Em.

'What do you mean? He's our dad, we'll recognise him.'

I wasn't so sure. I could picture big hands and hear a deep voice, that wasn't enough to go on.

I wasn't so sure of this and told Em so.

'Mum's got a picture,' my brother said. 'She showed me, that night . . . you know.'

I knew what night he meant, the night with all

the tears, the night we'd decided to get him back.

'She showed you? Why didn't she show me?' I said.

Em squinted at me. 'Did you ask?'

I stuck out my lip and shook my head. I didn't see why that made a difference, he was my dad too.

'Stop sulking, I'll get the photo,' my brother said, cramming another T-shirt into his bag. It was late now and our mother had been asleep for an hour at least.

'You'll get it?' I scoffed at my brother. 'You couldn't sneak if your life depended on it.'

'Shut up,' he replied, picking up one of my clumpy shoes from under the bed and hurling it at me. 'Mum's well gone by now and besides you don't know where it is.'

I threw the shoe back.

'Go on then,' I said.

I did recognise him, Em was right.

He was tall, almost gangly. His face was like my brother's and Grace's. I guess it was a bit like mine too, but I'd always looked a lot like Uncle Victor.

Mum was in the photo, too. They were standing

166

outside a small house, with some trees in the background. I didn't recognise the place.

'It's our grandmother's house,' Em told me. 'Mum says that Grace was already growing inside her too.'

I stared at my mother's stomach, no sign of the impending birth showed through the green dress she wore. They looked happy. Remy was smiling as she looked up at Céléstin. He looked like he'd just told a joke, staring into the camera with a grin. We needed to get him back.

'This is the most important thing we've got, Em.' I looked at my brother seriously.

Em grinned at me, looking even more like the man whose photo I held. 'Tuck it in your sock, then.' He laughed.

My sock already held all the money we had. Frankie's 'little something' had turned out to be fifty quid and I wanted to keep it extra safe.

Em thought I was being stupid. 'Who'd steal from two little African boys,' he said.

But I knew who. Once upon a time I would have stolen from two little African boys. And they were still out there, Kieran and Ibby, and tons more like them.

I carefully folded the picture and tucked it into

my empty left sock.

'Gimme the money,' Em said.

'It's safe here,' I replied.

'I've got socks too, come on.'

I handed it over and Em filled his sock, like me. I love my brother. He does anything to make me feel safe, even if it makes him feel stupid. That's a good brother, right?

We did sleep a bit. Em had worked out that we needed to be up at 4. My brother set the alarm on a digital watch I'd never seen before.

'I borrowed it,' he said when I stared. I knew what borrowed meant. Em's morals were not as inflexible as he'd want me to believe.

So, we slept a bit.

I woke up before the alarm. I didn't often have nightmares, but my pillow was damp with tears when I woke up that morning. I scrubbed my eyes, leapt off the bunk and shook my brother awake.

'We've got to leave a note,' I hissed.

In my nightmares, my mother had woken up the next morning alone, everyone gone. She'd lost her husband and now her sons were gone and even her baby, Grace. She'd wept and screamed and shouted at the ceiling.

We had to leave a note.

My brother opened one sleepy eye. 'I've done it,' he croaked.

'What? When?' I asked.

'I woke up too, earlier. I can't believe we didn't think of it before. Imagine what she would have felt like if she didn't know what had happened.' I had imagined, I didn't want to again. 'This is gonna hurt her enough,' Em continued. 'She'll be gutted.'

I thought about this for a moment. We were so desperate to make everyone happy, to put things back how they were, that we hadn't thought of this. Would tomorrow's happiness erase today's grief?

'Are we doing the right thing?' I asked.

Em stared at me, didn't reply for a long time. But when he did his answer was sure, firm, full of conviction. 'Yes,' he said.

I asked to see the note. He'd already put it in the kitchen, so we went through. The flat was dark and quieter than ever before. Normally you could hear the clomp of feet from above or the hum of a television below, but no one was up now.

Em got a glass of water while I read.

Dear Mum,

We know you won't understand what we're doing, but we've got to do it. We're going to get Dad. I write it now and it sounds silly. I know you'd stop us if we told you, but we've got to. It doesn't work without him, does it? We need him, you need him, Grace needs him. When you read this, we'll be on a plane. We will try to phone you when we arrive. I don't know what else to say, Mum. We've got to try.

Love, Em and Prince

I could see her reading it and it didn't change the nightmare much, only this time Grace was there, adding her cries to our mother's.

I scrawled my own message at the bottom.

I love you, Mum.

Em nodded over me. 'She'll like that, Prince,' he said.

I stared glumly at the paper and my doubt returned. *Will we break her heart again?* I thought. We had to get this right. My brother was right, we needed Dad, Mum needed him. He'd put it all back together again.

Em placed a hand on my shoulder.

'It's time,' he said.

Chapter 37

It was easy getting to the airport, Em had worked it all out. We needed to get on an empty night bus, then a train, and we were there. My brother had done some more "borrowing" to pay for this too.

'That fifty quid isn't gonna last long,' he said, then added, 'it's just borrowing, I will pay it back.' I believed he'd try. Like I'd try to pay back Jubrel. I didn't know how, but I'd try.

The bus roared down empty roads, stopping to pick up bleary-eyed passengers, and soon enough we were at the bright train station, lit up in contrast to the dark night. I'd not been to this one before, but there's something familiar about all big train stations, isn't there? More than the signs and the same newsagents tucked into the corners of all of them, there's something in the air, the vast expanse of air that flows around the terminus. You can feel it on your face.

I had a serious fright on the train.

Em thought we should make sure we had everything. 'Passports?' he said.

I pulled Jubrel's doctored one out of my trouser pocket and replied, 'Check.'

Em brandished his too before saying, 'Tickets?'

I fished around in the same pocket and finally waved the envelope at my brother.

'Money?' Em asked.

I tapped down my socks, nothing. I emptied them, no money, just a balled-up bus ticket. I started searching through my bag, a few clothes, a book. Em said I'd need for the plane, my toothbrush.

My brother was doing the same, frantically tearing through his few possessions. Then he started laughing.

'Sock,' he said. 'The money's in my sock.'

I breathed a sigh which quickly became a laugh too, a nervous laugh. I took the money back off him and stuffed it back in my sock. Later, I was very glad

I had done that.

The airport was busy. It was like entering the world again. People rushed everywhere, wheeling suitcases small and large. Men in yellow jackets swept and pushed giant metal trolleys to and fro.

We headed to the desk that bore the same logo as our tickets.

'Good morning,' a smiling woman said. Her hair was reddish and piled up on top of her head, I didn't know how it was held up there. 'Have you got tickets, boys?' she asked.

We mumbled a hello before I handed over the tickets.

'Hmm.' She looked concerned. 'You know that you're very late.'

I looked up at the clock that rested on the wall just above her head. It read 06:52. 'No,' I replied, panic rising. 'The plane's at seven-thirty, right?'

'That's right,' the woman said, nodding, her red hair bobbing backwards and forwards. 'You needed to be here two hours before departure.' She sounded like a teacher. 'You can check your bags here, then you'll have to run straight to passport control.'

I didn't know what she meant by check but Em grabbed my bag off my shoulder and thrust it down on the conveyor belt beside the woman. She handed us two more bits of paper that she called Boarding Passes before pointing further into the airport and saying, 'Go on then, run!'

Neither of us hesitated. We left our bags with the red-headed lady who was tying labels round the handles and sprinted into the hurrying crowd. We dodged and ducked our way, trying to read each sign as we hurtled past. I could hear Em shouting apologies as he collided with a few suitcases. I had a lead of ten, maybe fifteen metres when I sighted the long queue to pass through the security barriers of passport control. I didn't slow down but headed straight in. Several people stepped in behind me, before my brother, panting and sweating, joined the line too.

I passed back his ticket and boarding pass, then we waited. We waited for the test. Would our fake passports work? Or was this the end of the line?

We hadn't spared much breath to discuss whether they'd work. We both knew they were shoddy but we'd try anyway. I had, however, given more than a little time to thinking about what happened if they didn't. Visions of arrest swam before my eyes. This didn't really scare me, it was what happened afterwards, when they contacted the real owners of the passports.

I hated what I'd done to Jubrel. But it was the only way I knew, the only way to get my dad back. We needed him. Jubrel would understand that. I hoped Jubrel would understand that.

So we waited and I thought about my former foster carers and my long-lost dad, about how far we'd come and how far we still had to go.

Finally, no one stood between me and the line of booths, housing the people ready to check our passports. I stepped forward, pretending confidence.

The man who asked for my passport and ticket had a moustache, black-rimmed glasses and, to my pleasure, a glazed look in his eyes. He'd worked a long shift already, I guessed. He glanced down at the passport, at the ticket, then back up at me. I tensed every muscle in my body.

Out of the corner of my eye I could see my brother approaching a booth, two away from mine. He handed over his documents as I received mine back and my body relaxed. I walked forward, still watching my brother. His passport control officer, a woman with short cropped hair, opened her mouth. I was too distant to hear what she said. As I stepped towards the security gate, the lady turned away from Em and my brother turned too, turned and ran.

Chapter 38

Dar Es Salaam, Tanzania

Céléstin rapped at the door. It had been only a few short minutes since he'd watched Victor enter. He knew he was inside. He wasn't where he should be, he wasn't where he'd said he'd be, he wasn't looking after Emmanuel and me.

Céléstin had no patience and knocked again before Victor could have possibly answered it.

'I'm coming,' a voice boomed from the other side.

When the door swung open, Céléstin was ready. He leapt forward, grabbing his much larger sibling by the throat.

'Where are they?' he hissed, a man possessed.

'Brother,' Victor gasped, grappling with his older

sibling's arm, 'please, let me talk.'

'Where. Are. They?' Céléstin's words hung in the air and Victor stopped struggling.

Eventually he whispered a reply. 'I do not know.'

Another pause hung between them, so tense you could almost touch it. This one ended with a violent bout of coughing which forced Céléstin to release Victor's neck.

The large man looked out of the door, closed it, then led his still spluttering brother to a chair.

'I am sorry,' Victor said when Céléstin had recovered, 'I am so sorry, they . . . I . . . it was too much.'

Céléstin didn't reply but stared at his brother.

'We could not work,' Victor continued. 'We had no money. We had to live somehow. I became . . . someone else, brother, a criminal, a gangster. I still am.' Victor buried his face in his hands.

For a moment Céléstin's loyalties were split. Here was his brother, a broken man, yet he was the man who should be looking after his sons, the man who had promised.

Céléstin rose to his feet. 'What happened to them?' he growled, approaching his brother.

Victor looked up but did not rise from his own seat.

'It was me or them, brother. I am sorry. I am.'

Céléstin was right above him now and repeated his question. 'What happened to them?'

'I kicked them out. I do not know what happened. I am truly sorry, brother.'

Céléstin did not reply. He raised his fist, ready to strike his sibling with every ounce of strength. Victor did not raise a hand to defend himself. The blow began to fall when another fit of coughing racked my father's body. He doubled over, convulsing with each bark, blood spraying out across the floor and my uncle's shoes. Then my father collapsed.

Victor looked down at the blood and knew what it must mean. He carried his older brother through to his own bed, then made some phone calls.

He would put it right. He would put it all right, whatever the cost.

Chapter 39

For ages I sat on the plane, still on the runway.

After a while someone announced that there was a problem and that they had to remove some luggage. It was so hot that I could barely breathe, let alone think about what Em might be going through. I could only assume he'd been arrested and worry that the police would soon be boarding the plane to arrest me too.

It didn't help that the guy sitting next to me was sweating like he'd just finished a football match – he wasn't that fat either. Why do some people sweat so much? A little while later the lady on the plane brought us all a little bottle of water, about half the size of a proper bottle of water. The not-too-fat guy gulped his down in one shot. I sipped.

The take-off was the worst bit. Not-too-fat-sweats-a-lot had started to stink the place up which made me gag, then the plane was moving, lifting off the ground, accelerating, and my stomach felt like someone was using it to mix a cake in. My head pounded too. I tried closing my eyes, but then I could see my brother being dragged away so I opened them again.

When the plane seemed to calm down a bit, I could think only one thing. *Can I do this alone?*

I knew that the ideas had been mine. I knew that I'd had to drag Em along half the time. I knew that we wouldn't have got this far without me. But Em held me together, he kept me on the right path, he stopped me from doing anything too stupid. And now he was gone. It was just me. Alone.

The flight wasn't like in films where you watch a little television and get served meals on little trays. We did eat, but it was a sandwich, cheese and salad, an apple and another miniature bottle of water. The guy next to me bought a bottle of beer and drank loudly as he listened to tinny-sounding music.

All of this filtered through me as I thought about what I would do next. Our plans had got us this far. I was on my way to Tanzania. But I knew, when the plane landed, a whole city awaited, a whole city in which I needed to find one man, a needle in a big box of needles.

The touch-down was horrific too. I was so worked up from worrying about being alone and how I could find my father, that I began to breathe funny, as if someone was strangling me. It was so bad that Not-too-fat-sweats-a-lot-slurps-when-he-drinks took his headphones out long enough to ask if I was OK. I told him I was fine.

By the time we'd actually stopped and people started to get off the plane I think I was fine, at least fine-ish.

I've got this far, I said to myself. It hadn't gone one hundred per cent to plan, but I was nearly in Tanzania. I could do the rest. I was fine.

Until I saw passport control, that is. My breath caught and I stopped on the balls of my feet, staring ahead. The other passengers poured past me, heading for the little lines.

Last hurdle, I thought and lurched forward.

It was nothing like London.

'Next!' The man called. He was sitting behind a little desk, not in his own booth.

'Passport,' he said, when I approached.

He flicked through it saying, 'Good, good, good, goo-ood,' then stamped one of the pages with a big square stamp.

'OK, visa?' he said next.

'Visa?' I replied. This was a brand-new word to me. The last of my fine-ness quickly evaporated.

'Visa, visa,' he repeated impatiently. A queue of people was forming and I had the same strangling feeling I'd had on the plane.

Last hurdle and I'd stumbled. I shrugged at the man, defeated.

Now, if you're like me, you won't know what a visa is either. I've found out now, so I'll tell you. It's nothing special, it's just a form thing which says that you're allowed to go into such and such a country. You have to pay for it. Money, that's all it takes. It's like an extra tax for tourists.

I didn't know any of this. So when the passport man said, 'Money, money, quick,' I was surprised, but did what he said.

I pulled the money out from my sock. The man grabbed it and took the two twenty pound notes. That left me ten pounds. I didn't dare say anything.

Then, with my money in his hand, he called out, 'Next!' and turned away from me.

That was it, I couldn't believe it. I snatched up my passport and fled.

On the plane, I'd had vague ideas about finding a hotel first, but with so little money left that seemed unlikely. Next I thought I'd find a police station or something like that, and see if they could help, but I was so shaken up by the visa incident that I didn't dare go to the police. Finally, I thought I would hire a taxi. A taxi driver would know the city, would know where the gangsters were, might have even seen the tall man whose photo was nestled inside my other sock. But, again, the money was all but gone.

A new plan didn't strike me as I half-walked, half-ran away from passport control.

Nothing came as I waited to collect my bag, or as I lugged it towards the exits.

Still my mind was blank when I walked through the nearest doors.

Out I stepped into the blazing African sun and straight into a man I hadn't thought I'd ever see again.

Chapter 40

Back in London

'Can you just wait here a moment?' said the woman with the short cropped hair.

Em didn't wait, he turned and walked at an ever-quickening pace. He wasn't stupid. My brother knew his passport was a fake and he knew what came next.

Before long he was running through the airport, staying near the walls, keeping his eyes on as many people as he could. No one seemed to be following.

Later, he told me that he knew I'd keep going, he knew that I'd get there on my own, he knew that I'd do all I could to bring back our father. He also knew that it wouldn't help if he was arrested. So he fled the airport as quickly as possible.

It didn't take long, the return journey. Train, bus, walk. Em said that it seemed even shorter than the way there.

He arrived at the flats at about the time we'd normally get up, so he was surprised to hear a deep voice vibrating through the door. He didn't enter straight away but listened a moment.

'Are they here?'

'Why should I tell you anything? Get out, get out!' Mother's pleading tone urged Em to put his key into the lock.

'Are your boys here, woman?' was the last thing my brother heard as he pushed open the door, rushed down the hall and slammed through the kitchen door.

He took everything in. Mum was sitting at the table, her face streaked with dirty tears, her cheeks glowing red. In her right hand she clutched the note we had placed there a few hours before. Above her stood a man. Darker in skin than us, tall, but not massive, he wore a black bomber jacket, zipped up. Grace was nowhere to be seen.

'Leave her alone!' Em shouted.

'They are here,' the man said, for some reason clearly relieved. 'Listen to . . .'

Em wasn't prepared to listen. 'Who are you?' he said, at the same time as Mum screamed, 'Emmanuel, you stupid boy!' Then she leapt up and threw herself at her son, the invader forgotten.

'You are all mad,' the man muttered as my brother was drowned in a barrage of hugs, blows, kisses, tears and cross words.

Em spent at least half an hour trying to calm Mum down. She was furious with my brother and me.

'Stupid, stupid boys,' she said again and again, fresh tears blooming in her large eyes. Eventually, Grace woke up and Remy had to go and fetch her.

All this time the man had waited.

'Listen,' he said as soon as our mum left the room. 'I am so pleased to find you here. I just have a message, for you or your mother. It is from Victor.'

Em's face darkened at the mention of our wicked uncle, the man who had cast us out, who had sent us to live amongst thieves.

'I don't want to hear anything from him,' my brother replied.

'He said that if I found you, you would not want to hear from him,' the man continued. 'But this is important, boy. Victor said I must find you or I would regret it. He works for some dangerous guys, you know.'

My brother opened his mouth to protest again.

'No, no, just listen. He's with your father.' Em's mouth quickly snapped shut. 'In Dar Es Salaam. You must phone him, he says, it is urgent.'

Em's mouth opened, then closed again.

'I have a number.' The man filled the silence. 'Here.' He handed Em a piece of card, the corner torn off a cereal packet perhaps. 'You call him, OK? Tell him, Jimmy delivered the message. You remember that. Jimmy.' Then the man left, pulling at his zip, as if to draw the coat even tighter round his neck.

A moment of thought passed, filled with surprise, then Em picked up the phone, a small smile on his lips.

Chapter 41

Uncle Victor. His face loomed large in my nightmares, twisted with anger. The last time I had seen him, more than a year ago, he'd beaten Em bloody. He had sent us away like lambs amongst wolves.

Now, here he was again. He formed a dark silhouette, the sun blocked out behind him. I turned to run. He could do me no good, I thought. But his arm snaked, his hand gripped my wrist, the same hand that had once tried to strangle me.

He was trying to talk to me, but the blood careering through my veins, pounding in my ears, dulled any sound he made. I cried out, but no one gave us a second glance. A child throwing a tantrum is probably what they saw, not a boy abandoned to fear.

Eventually, a word rang through the pulse of blood. 'Father,' my uncle said urgently. I stopped pulling away, stood and looked down. I couldn't look in his face yet. 'Your father, Céléstin. Prince, he's here. Your father's here.'

Now I looked up, not to the monster of my daydreams, but to my uncle.

'You are here to get him, Prince,' Victor said.

I frowned at him. How had he known this?

'I spoke to your brother, Prince, on the telephone. He told me that you were coming but I thought I would miss you. I am so pleased that I did not.'

I wasn't sure if I agreed yet. Finally I spoke, my pulse slowing. 'The plane was delayed.'

My uncle nodded but asked no questions. 'Come, Prince, we must go,' he said.

He pulled at my arm. I didn't budge.

Victor turned and looked at me, his eyes filled, not with anger but with anguish. 'He is very ill, Prince,' he said in the quietest voice I'd ever heard my uncle use. 'We must go. I should not leave him long.'

I was lost. This was all too much to take in. I allowed my uncle to drag me along, my mind a blur.

Soon we were speeding away from the airport in

a rattling car. Beads hung from the rear-view mirror and the doorless glove-box was stuffed with newspapers. The passing sights, the heat, the dust, the one-storey buildings stirred up long-forgotten memories of Africa.

I turned to my uncle from the passenger seat. 'My father is ill?' I asked.

Victor didn't take his eyes off the road. Other motorists, in cars, on motor-bikes, in vans and buses, swerved in and out of the traffic, seemingly fearless.

'He's very ill, Prince,' he said.

A bicycle cut in front of us and Victor touched the brakes as he sounded the horn. The cyclist paid him no heed. I barely noticed, I was gathering courage to ask my next question.

'Is he dying?' I said, my voice cracking through the vital word.

'We will not let him die, my nephew. What I think he has, what he surely has, they can treat. In Britain they can treat it very easily. You must do what you came for, you must take him back with you.'

I was expecting my uncle to take us to a hospital but I was wrong. His flat was sparsely furnished, but clean. The first room we entered had a few chairs, a small kitchen area and a high slit of window that cast only a little light. It was cool compared to the blistering heat outside, and the sweat that clung to my back began to chill me. A doorway was set in the far wall, a thin curtain hanging in front of it.

From the second room, a hacking cough could be heard, an uncontrolled bark, its low pitch muffled by a cloth or a hand.

Then a voice rose, deep, as I remembered it, measured like my brother, tugging at me.

'Are you back, Victor?' my father called.

Chapter 42

I've never run faster than when I heard that voice. I pushed the curtain to one side and blinked back the tears that I didn't know I'd even shed.

'Dadda!' I croaked.

The tall man, so like my brother, lay on a thin mattress, covered with a threadbare blanket. He quickly rose, his eyes never leaving mine. 'My Prince, my Prince, is it really you?'

He crossed the room in two long strides. I dissolved in his arms. I was a child again, a toddler, a baby. And I knew that we were right – we needed him. I needed him.

For a long time we stood as tears swamped both

our faces. We would hug, then pull away, looking into each other's eyes, only to embrace again. All the while my father whispered. 'My Prince, my boy.'

I said nothing. I'd thought a lot about what I would say to my father if we ever met again. But when it comes to it, what we plan to say and what comes out of our mouths are two very different things.

Eventually, we were interrupted by a cough, not the hacking fit my father had suffered earlier, but a gentle 'Ahem'. Victor stood in the doorway.

'I have to do one thing,' he said, 'then you must go.' He gave us no chance to respond but turned and left. And finally I had a chance to catch my breath. Everything had happened so quickly. I couldn't believe that my father was there, that I could reach out and touch him.

He pulled me close again and spoke to the top of my head. 'Let us go and sit,' he said.

His arm round my shoulders, we walked back through the curtain into the dimly lit room. My father fell heavily into one of the wooden chairs; I perched.

'I cannot believe that you are here, my son,' my father said, echoing my own thoughts. 'It has been a long time.'

I did not know what to say. How to explain all that

had happened, how to put years into words, I did not know. How to condense sadness, pain, anger, loss and hope into a few sentences, I did not know. So I did not speak, I just stared at my father.

'You have come a long way, my boy.' My father smiled a broad smile at me, his eyes still red from the tears. 'Victor says you have come to take me home.'

'We need you,' I blurted as if to excuse the lengths we'd gone to and as the words escaped I knew that I'd said all I needed to. We needed him.

Our tears began to fall again.

'I am sorry,' my father said, 'I am sorry for everything. I'm sorry that we had to send you away, sorry that I've not been there. Sorry for what Victor did to you.' I blinked in surprise. 'Yes, your uncle has told me everything. Don't forget I am his big brother. I am sorry, my son. You and Emmanuel have had to be so brave. And now I am even more sorry that I cannot come with you.'

I was shocked. 'You must . . .' I began but my father quickly interrupted.

'With all of my heart, I wish that I could, Prince. But there are men here who I owe a lot of money to. They have people in London too, men who could hurt you all. I will not have that.'

'But you are sick, father,' I pleaded.

'Damn that man,' my father cursed. 'I told Victor not to speak of it.'

My father fixed me with his dark eyes, a swirl of black and brown, deep as a well.

'I must keep you safe, you, Emmanuel, your mother, Grace. The only way for me to do that is to stay, to repay my debts.'

I argued. I begged. I wept. But I knew I could not move him. I had come this far only to have the life I wanted, longed for, snatched away by the one person who could give it to me.

My father tried to turn the conversation to Grace and Emmanuel. 'How are they?' 'How big is Grace now?' 'Is Remy OK?' But he could not move me either. I could be as stubborn as he.

I gazed at him, trying to remember every hair on his head, the red-brown stains on his long white dress, the pattern of dark freckles across his nose, features I now feared I would never see again.

When the front door opened, Victor entered a room heavy with tension.

'We are set,' he said. 'We must go now.'

'I have told you, Victor, I cannot go. My place is here. It is the only way.'

My mouth tightened at my father's continued protests. It could not be the only way. Bile rose in my throat.

'I have money,' my uncle said, and finally my father and I turned to look at Victor.

'Here,' he said, holding up a thick wedge of cash held together with a red rubber band. 'It is enough, it will get you there, brother. You . . .'

But Victor did not get to finish his sentence. The door once again creaked open. Sweat appeared on my uncle's brow instantly and my father lurched into another coughing fit.

Through the doorway came three men, whom both my father and his brother definitely recognised. Two of them were almost as big as my uncle, broad and tall. The other could not have been taller than Em. All three wore suits. Despite their size the two larger men's clothing was far too big, their jackets hanging like dressing gowns. The shortest of the three wore a suit that was razor sharp, clearly made just for him. His beard was cut to a fine point too.

'I knew something was up, Victor. You have been with us, what, three months? You have not missed a day.' The menace on the larger men's faces was clear but the short one spoke casually. 'And now we find you like this, eh, big-man.'

Victor's mouth flopped open but it was my father who spoke. 'Please,' he said, 'let the boy go. He does not need to be here.'

The small man's casual tone continued. 'I don't believe that I spoke to you, Mr Anatole,' he said, then raised a finger. One of the two huge thugs stepped across the room and struck a blow to my father's face that froze me to my seat.

'Leave my brother alone,' Victor shouted, moving towards Célestin. But he did not reach him. The second henchman grabbed his large arms and the one that had struck my father planted an even fiercer blow into Victor's stomach.

My father was slouched in the chair, and now my uncle doubled over as the small man laughed.

'Brother!' he said. 'This is priceless! Who's the boy then?' I didn't dare look at him, not directly. 'Let me guess . . . son?' Victor began to straighten up. 'But whose?' the man continued.

Another finger was raised and guns were drawn from over-sized jackets. Heavy metal pieces aimed at my uncle and at me.

'It matters not,' the sharp-suited menace continued. 'Get rid of the boy, he's worthless. This one still has his debt to repay,' he said, nodding towards my still-slumped father. 'And show Victor what happens to traitors.' With that he turned to go, leaving us with our executioners.

Chapter 43

I'm not ashamed to say that I wet myself. I defy you to say that you would not.

'NO!' my uncle screamed. 'The debt, let me pay the debt.'

The short man stopped, turned and looked from my uncle to my father.

'An interesting proposal. You'll certainly make more money than this wheezing old man. You know what it means for you?' My uncle nodded. 'You won't be leaving this town,' he nodded again, 'ever!' Pretensions of casualness left the room, true menace stalked that word.

'The debt is mine,' Victor said. 'I owe them both

more than you know.'

My father had begun to straighten his head as the short man spoke again. 'You have stolen from me too, Victor,' he said pointing at the money that my uncle still clutched. 'You owe me. You know what we do to thieves?'

Victor nodded a third time.

The two brutes laughed, the guns went away and they grabbed at Victor. A heavy knife appeared in one of their hands as the other pulled up my uncle's sleeve, holding his arm out straight.

Tears joined the sweat pooling on my uncle's face. 'Let them go,' he said.

The short man nodded. 'Am I not kind to you, Victor?' He laughed again, grabbed the money from Victor's free hand and threw it at me. 'Am I not kind, boy?'

I looked at the still laughing man, at the knife, at my uncle. 'Get out!' Victor roared at me for the second time in my life. 'Take your father and go.' The first time he had said those words had been the worst act of cruelty I'd ever suffered. This day, he made amends.

The monster from my nightmares was gone, replaced by my uncle.

My knees shook as I rose and I would not have

been able to hold my father if he had not regained consciousness. We staggered from the flat.

I tried to forget the sounds that followed us out, the wet thud, my uncle's piercing scream, the wicked, stupid laughter. But they rang in my ears through our journey to the airport. My father could barely speak, he moaned and held his head as a taxi sped us back through the dark city. My time in Dar Es Salaam had already come to an end.

I ignored my return ticket and booked us both on the next plane back, using my uncle's stolen money. As the airport lady handed over the slips of paper, I thanked Victor under my breath.

It was a long wait for the plane and my father started to stir. We talked for several hours as we sat, and it was just like chatting with my brother. I told him about the family: Mum, Grace and Em. He coughed, the same hacking cough that I'd heard back in the flat. We did a bit of shopping too, food, drink; even at night, airports never close. I found a bear with a bright blue ribbon for Grace. We didn't mention what had happened.

As the sun rose, we boarded a plane.

You might have some questions at this point. If you don't, then I don't think you've been reading carefully enough.

Number 1: What happened to your luggage? Good question. Strangely, I don't know the answer. My best guess is that I left it in Uncle Victor's car.

Number 2: Didn't Céléstin need a passport? Yes, he did. Thankfully, my father was more prepared than I have shown myself to be; he had kept this important document on his person since he'd left his mother's house months before.

'I thought I might need it in a hurry,' he said. 'And I was right.'

Number 3: Did you change your trousers? Well, I lost the luggage, right? So, you take a guess.

The shaking started on the plane. Uncontrollable shudders ran through my body, though I wasn't cold. The lady on the plane brought me a blanket, and my father wrapped it around me and held me tight. Later, someone told me this sometimes happens when scary, sad or unexpected things happen. I think I could claim all of those.

Dawn came on fast, my shaking ceased and I slept through the rest of the flight. We arrived in London a day after I'd left. It felt like a year.

I led my father through the city, by train and bus. I led him back to his family. I led him to where he was needed.

Chapter 44

Summer came, and with it lush green grass that covered our park. We held ice-creams in our hands, me, Em and my dad, as we kicked a scratched football back and forth, the forged signature all but obliterated.

'We've got to get a new ball, boys,' my dad called as he popped the last of his cone into his mouth and received a well directed pass from Emmanuel.

He coughed, just once. The treatment was working and the doctors were sure he'd make a full recovery. He passed the ball on to me, hard and fast along the ground. I flicked it up as it arrived and caught it on my new trainers, the fluorescent green tick lurid against the grass. Even after buying back Jubrel's gun, my uncle's blood money still stretched far.

'Very clever, Princey.' From the nearest bench, my mum shouted out. She was sharing an ice-cream with a curly-haired Grace, who in turn was sharing it with her bear. The poor teddy had to be washed every few weeks; Grace wouldn't be parted from it, no matter how many toys she got.

After flicking the ball up again I volleyed it back to my father, who trapped it under his foot with ease; it was clear where I got my football skills from.

'Come and get it then, slow-coaches,' he shouted, then ran with the ball at his feet.

I shared a glance and a huge grin with my brother, turned and chased after my dad. We ran until the sweat poured down our faces, until our lungs burned and the green grass was churned up beneath our feet. We followed the defaced ball, desperate to keep it at our feet as long as possible. Taunting one another made it even more enjoyable.

'I've still got some tricks,' my brother hollered as he took the ball from our dad and tried to skip away.

Emmanuel was good, but my dadda was better. He laughed and laughed as he took the ball back, threaded it between my legs, and spun past us.

'You can do better than that!' he called in his deep voice.

That's how we play football, my dadda, Emmanuel and me.

After ten minutes or so, we collapsed on the ground, me and my brother either side of our dad.

'You know, boys,' he reached out and took hold of our hands, 'I'm a blessed man.'

And me?

Well, even after all that's happened, I know I'm blessed too. And, finally, I'm happy.

TOM AVERY lives in North London with his wife
and two bouncing boys. When he's not writing,
he works as a teacher in a Camden school.
His debut novel, *Too Much Trouble*, won the
Frances Lincoln Diverse Voices Book Award in 2010.

"This prize-winning story will grab readers' attention
from the opening moments and hold them
spellbound from then on."
Julia Eccleshare – Lovereading